THE PROSECUTOR
Ahmet Prençi

Princ Press— Minneapolis, MN
ISBN: 979-8-218-53188-1
eBook ISBN: 979-8-3305-4290-1
Library of Congress Control Number: 2024921964
Title: *The Prosecutor*
Author: Ahmet Prençi
Digital distribution | 2024
Paperback | 2024

This is a work of fiction. The characters, names, incidents, places, and dialogue are products of the author's imagination, and are not to be construed as real.

Translator Albanian to English by June Taylor
Reviewed by the editing team at New Book Authors Publishing

Published in the United States by New Book Authors Publishing

"Only those capable of envisaging utopia will be fit for the decisive battle, that of recovering all the humanity we have lost"
--Ernesto Sabato

Chapter I
A blast from the past

For Prosecutor Martin Guri, that afternoon should have been a routine moment of winding down as official working hours drew to a close. But, all of a sudden, the foreseeable flow of events is upturned, converting into a hologram that instantly jumbles all your coordinates, ties you down, hand and foot, mind and mouth, suspending you over a yawning abyss of nothingness.

It even felt as if the office walls with their tall windows, the ceiling, and the floor were closing in on him, restraining him, body and soul. The heavy office chair spun on its axis. Grabbing hold of the edge of the desk, he teetered forward as if walking on clouds of cotton wool. He swayed towards a nearby armchair and slumped into it like a chain-sawed oak tree.

Only after collapsing into the armchair did he realize that the windows and walls were stationary. But he still felt a heavy weightiness on his chest. Instinctively, he placed the palm of his right hand over his heart. He felt the heat diffuse throughout his chest like hot steam and the clamminess of cold sweat on the back of his neck.

The human hologram and sorceress, the mysterious woman, glided silently out of Prosecutor Maritn Guri's office and left him sprawled there like Pompeii after the Eruption.

Arjana, or "the blast from the past," as Martin later called her, had requested an appointment according to protocol but without providing a reason. "I wish to discuss a private matter with the Prosecutor," she had declared to Security and the secretarial staff. She showed no signs of being a person who could cause problems. Quite the opposite, her striking looks and politeness had favourably impressed the personnel at the entrance and exit to the Grave Crime Prosecution Offices.

To Martin, however, she resembled a Deity from Antiquity, who expires and is resurrected on the same day, a stark black shadow that bites and injects venom where it hurts you the most. The words she uttered, the message she brought, the way she exited the office, her elegant appearance, the stunning portrait, an almost magical silvery aureole about her, the long hair and penetrating gaze metamorphosed her into the most unfathomable being, akin to those that meander at their leisure between existence and non-existence, between Heaven and Earth, messengers between the World above and the World below.

"She is so like those ancient Greek goddesses," Martin rambled, returning to his senses.

To protect her son from his father, who wanted to devour him, Rhea, daughter of Uranus and Gaia, consort of Cronus and mother of Zeus, gave birth to him deep in a cave on Crete. Instead of her son, Rhea gave Cronus a stone swathed in infant's sheets. Cronus fell for his consort's trick and, hence, Zeus was saved…

Possibly for the first time in his career, Martin was in no shape to go home. He did not have it in him, and he did not have the desire to. From the moment Arjana stepped into his office, spilling out an account and an ultimatum connected to a long-forgotten event thirty years ago, he felt as though the bastion of his life suddenly resembled a structure that had been stormed and ravished by some lightning-fast power that radiated menacing, annihilating, and lethal energy.

"If what the newspapers and television are claiming about my son is in those files, then that is devastating beyond words, and I cannot stand back and allow you to use them. If you do not doctor what is in these files, I will not speak to you as I am today! This whole thing, this truth, will weigh fair and square on your shoulders because, in my situation, I have nothing to lose. See to it that this is taken care of before I speak to you again. If you fail to do what I am asking of you today, rest assured I will not be using the language I am using now. Get it done before it's too late and the world finds out all about you. Do it for your good as well,"! she had said decisively, cold and calculated, pulling the door lightly shut behind her.

Lying on the desktop were thick files resembling derelict stone border markers. A frozen image pulsated on the computer screen. A pungent smell arose from a pile of quashed cigarette butts in an ashtray a few inches further over. A haze of cigarette smoke floated above the head and shoulders of the prosecutor like a lifeless amoeba. Everything in that office now seemed suffocating.

Several minutes had elapsed before he remembered to call his wife. He felt in total disarray. He curtly notified his assistant that he was free to go home. He hung up, and for a split second, his gaze came to rest on the photographs arranged neatly on his desk.

All his thoughts, plans, desires, goals, and ambitions seemed meaningless to him now. Just like that, his day-to-day reality rolled up and pulled from beneath his feet, laying bare a pathway towards a most challenging judgment in the days ahead.

Martin's eyes wandered back to the two photographs in their elegant frames that had been sitting on his desk for some time now. To the right was the family photo with his wife and two sons, and in the middle was a photograph of his friend, Artur Rrasa. The family photograph was a memento taken two years ago at a New Year's party. The shot was taken with the four of them seated, exchanging wishes, full of laughter and joy, especially the boys. Whereas, in the other photograph, he and Artur stood side by side, smiling complaisantly, chiefly due to the coaxing of the photographer…However, no matter how fleetingly awkward the moment, that smile now kept Artur alive in his heart. The snapshot had been taken one week before he was treacherously executed. These photographs served as two sturdy pillars of reference that Prosecutor Martin Guri would often return to during his work day. He drew strength from them, inspiration, and motivation to move forward with foresight, impartiality, wisdom, professionalism, courage, and respect for everything surrounding him, inside and outside this office. This is why these photos were always within his sight during the long periods he spent in his office. They always compelled him to pause and reflect, to be level-headed, unwavering, and compassionate in his decisions.

The photo of Artur Rrasa, his dear friend and unforgettable colleague, kept the memory of him alive and fresh. To him, the principles of his mission were sacrosanct, and he defended them as such. He stared intently at the face behind the glass in the frame, and instantly, his mind was transported back in time. Somewhat unnatural this leap from, "If you fail to alter these materials, I will certainly not be using the same language with you that I am today," - to Artur.

The scene of the shooting, the bullets, Artur's body slumped there on the footpath, and the immense weight of death, which he had never even imagined like this, either for him or himself, suddenly sprung to mind and subtly diffused throughout his whole being in the wake of Arjana's departure.

He wondered why he had created the impression that if he were to squeeze that woman hard enough, nothing but venom would ooze out of her. The core of her ultimatum projected verbal bullets that left the prosecutor reeling. He had often heard the expression, "Words slay, like bullets," but had never really given it much thought. Furthermore, as part of a prosecutor's functions, penalties dispensed (naturally, in words) were, undoubtedly, a "bullet" for someone. Still, Martin always raised the shield of the law for protection, and things never went as far as a "bullet word" for the other party. Now, it was his turn to discover how much pain a "bullet-word" inflicted when Arjana imposed such a harsh ultimatum.

She entered and exited the office; her eyes seemed lifeless, but there was an almost murderous glint to them. In that split-second, it felt as if he had swapped places with his best friend, and it was he who had taken the bullets and was lying crumpled on the ground. That was the most shocking experience of life inverted. What if it had been him who had died, not Artur? At least this day, like today, would never have happened; he wouldn't have had to go through such a harrowing dilemma, and that woman would never have been able to appear before him this way ever... *Maybe I am on their lists; perhaps they have planned an ambush this evening using Arjana as an alibi?* With these thoughts in mind, he leaned over in his seat, lighting another cigarette. After filling his lungs with the white smoke, he released it with a deep sigh and watched absently as it spiralled upwards into the overhanging smoke cloud.

He had never felt that kind of vulnerability before. It was like an unconditional capitulation. Out of the question! This moment had nothing in common with Martin's world and personality; it was like some underhand, emotional, and complex game designed specifically for him. He felt he was under attack from a Trojan Horse in whose belly Arjana had concealed a treacherous army.

Earlier that afternoon, he had no idea that the mysterious woman who had requested an appointment was Arjana or that she had the distinct intention of dealing him a final blow. At first, he thought this was an absurd request coming from the unhinged mind of some woman.

For Martin, his family was his one shrine of peace, always waiting for him long after extended working hours. It is there, and only there, that he returns to life and love in the bona fide meaning of these words. Work was relentless stress, daily, plagued with emergencies and dramas of people who either breached the law or sought its protection.

He had a habit of never trying to justify himself on the phone by saying things like, *almost there, won't be long, on my way.* He considered these as pointless add-ons. Whatever happens, happens. To constantly remain captive of the unexpected was suicidal. He respected the professional code of a prosecutor, and his wife knew this only too well. His children were likewise accustomed to his very late or unexpected arrivals. However, when he crossed that threshold, he felt the exhilaration of indispensable family life. The exhaustion and pressures of the day lifted as if by magic; he felt at ease and calm in the presence of those he cherished and who meant everything to him. The night was falling, and darkness slowly swallowed up everything. Outside, it was cold. Beyond the glass panes, an inky blackness. Only the leafless branches of the beech trees could be detected, stiff silhouettes faintly illuminated by the reflections of city lights. Winter, which showed no signs of wanting to leave, whiplashed everything with benumbing cold. The season's icy mantel encased the naked branches and tree trunks, the empty streets and pavements, and people, too, who scattered like frightened birds, scurrying off in search of the welcoming warmth of their shelters. You could see the odd passer-by hurrying along, impatient to escape the cold of the falling dusk. The traffic had thinned out on the city streets and its growl was fading as if the vehicles were fleeing somewhere far off.

It was expected that this would be a very long night for Martin. His meeting with Arjana that afternoon and the unexpected conversation with her had shocked him to the core of his being.

That morning, she presented herself to the staff on duty at the Citizens' Reception Desk and asked for a meeting with Prosecutor Martin Guri. On receiving this routine request, he had cast an eye over his agenda and slotted in a meeting for 15:30. He phoned to confirm this meeting to the respective desk after checking that nothing clashed with the rest of his working hours.

The identity she had given said nothing to him, but he was intrigued by the motivation "for a private reason." So, he decided to meet her following the day's trial sittings, which was routine procedure for him when citizens asked to meet regarding issues not connected with cases under investigation.

The moment Arjana stepped into his office, the first thing that caught his attention were those beautiful eyes that so swiftly launched daggers at him. He had never seen eyes like that before; they drew you in involuntarily. Even though slightly hooded and set back in that smooth, white forehead, and although circled by several delicate lines, those eyes blazed, they flecked with several hues of unusual tints. He noted that perhaps she wore lenses. No, it wasn't that. Those eyes had existed for decades, just like that, beautiful, ice-cold, magnetic, and mysterious. He couldn't explain it, but that stare hit him like an energy field emitted from some unidentified object, the blinding flash of an unforeseen atomic blast. He should have focused on this unknown citizen's concern, not those iridescent eyes. *Deadly eyes,* he thought to himself, recalling the title of a popular novel, "Death comes to me from eyes like these." Could it be that death finds me too from eyes like this? he mused, concealing any indication of this train of thought, from his interlocutor.

Oddly enough, the conversation he had with Arjana brought him face to face with a moment in time connecting the two of them…A circumstance that he had completely forgotten about but which Arjana had not!

Ignorant of the issue the citizen was going to bring up, Martin Guri stuck to professional etiquette, creating every possibility for her to speak freely and at her ease without impediments or questions. Flipping a pen between his fingers, a gift from Artur, he gave the impression that he would duly take note of everything she would raise during this appointment. The woman spoke slowly but deliberately, with great care, preserving a respectful distance from the state official sitting before her. At first, he didn't understand a thing and found his attention was wavering.

Suddenly, he was all eyes and ears. Her story bore Martin many years back in time. This woman, seated across the desk from him in her black attire, her jet-black hair neatly tied back, and her pale and drawn face spirited him back to sequences from an old film he had almost forgotten about. Her story, with its two characters who happened to find themselves in the same place at the same time, began to torment him. Arjana was drawing him into a maze of complications. After revealing everything to the end, she didn't wait for a counter-reaction, for arguments, justifications, circumvention, an invitation for further discussion, and she was utterly disinterested in the state of mind of her interlocutor. She simply up and left the office, leaving in her wake a prosecutor with a noose over his head. She had seeded the sinister shadow of those words. She had dragged back into the present something that had happened but which Martin had long since erased from memory. That event transformed the prosecutor into a different being altogether. He remained rooted to the spot in his office, petrified, wordless like a fallen tree trunk.

Together with the dreams of very early youth, he had buried the incident with Arjana deep down in his memory. He couldn't even come up with a single explanation for himself. It had been thirty years. Martin had erased memories of the first and last time he met Arjana. However, as ill luck would have it, she resurfaced with a past to knock the present and the future into oblivion. That story blackened and overturned everything surrounding him. Everything he had painstakingly worked for all his life was seismically shaken up like the collision of tectonic plaques that, after many lethargic years, suddenly snatch away and swallow up people and buildings alike with apocalyptic momentum. Scientists say that volcanoes and earthquakes have definite periods of slumber and times of awakening. In those first few moments, he had not recognized Arjana. What had happened to the woman? How could she have undergone such a transformation? Is it reasonable to think that she, too, had been drawn into that obsessive craze some women have for plastic surgery? He knew that there were artists, singers, Members of Parliament, the wives of top-ranking politicians in Tirana who had undergone plastic surgery… *Arjana's made-over eyes,* he whispered to himself and stood up to pour himself a glass of whiskey, something he rarely did. He threw back the liquid in the thick, crystal glass in big gulps, staring vacantly into the darkness outside the windows. With his left hand, he scratched the back of his head at the base of his skull, a habit from childhood whenever he felt uneasy about something. Having returned to the black leather armchairs placed at the entrance to the office, he stared, in a daze, at the big swivel chair and the imposing worktable and beyond to the tall windows with their partly drawn beige curtains.

The shelving attached to the walls around him groaned beneath the weight of large volumes of codes and commentaries, law books, files, official newspapers, albums, and souvenirs neatly arranged along the edges of the solid wooden bookshelves. Nestled into the corner created between two armchairs was a globe of the world, temporarily mounted on a tiny corner table. Martin liked giving the globe a spin, secretly marveling at the enormous expanse of the world brought together over the rounded surface of this multicoloured sphere, like a toy. It made him slip back into the warm recollections of travel stories, events, and memories.

He had always enjoyed traveling.

Were we born to travel, or were we born to die? he asked himself on an impulse.

He believed that the act of leaving has always been and remains a mystery to humankind. Without this instinct, we would never have become what we are; without the adventure of leaving, we would have forever feared lands we could have inhabited. Thanks to all the departing, he gently caressed the globe like an apple.

He felt, deep down, the urge to bite into an apple. He always kept apples in the office. He opened the fridge and reached for one. *Apples from Dibra,* he murmured, holding the fresh, juicy fruit in his hand. *Life's destination is death, like the forbidden apple in the Book of Beginnings.* He was astonished at where that troubling idea sprung from that plunged him headlong into insane thoughts. *Life's destination is Death,* he muttered under his breath. The thought terrified him. He had never been known for theorizing. He was a prosecutor who tracked down "the predators of death," individuals who, with their savagery, slaughtered, stole, defiled, and struck terror into the hearts of others. He disputed this destination: Death. Was it not Martin Guri who pits the Law against these animal instincts of man? Was Martin Guri not in the process of building up the file on one of the hottest cases of the day? What him?! Yes, him! No one has cracked the mystery of death, the moment when, or the circumstances in which it may happen…

A scary silence had settled around him that evening in that office full of smoke, vapours from the air conditioning, and the fumes of the alcohol he was drinking. It was rare for him to consume alcohol, but he was a prolific smoker. He drifted mentally, confused and in shock, spinning in complicated spirals that he thought he would not be capable of exiting. The quietness surrounding him clashed with his state of mind; everything churned and tumbled around in his mind, everything - happenings, stories, memories, the past, his career, battles, victories, love, hate, failure…He felt everything evaporate in the vapor of that afternoon encounter with a woman with fake eyes, Arjana. Deep within, he felt nothing but horrific commotion and chaos.

He was one of the most experienced prosecutors in that imposing building in the capital. His career spanned twenty-seven years; briefly, he was an investigator with the Judicial Police. Then, he was promoted to the head of this unit and, later, to the position of prosecutor. All this had hardened and tested him. He had won high acclaim for the top priority cases he had worked on.

He was known for his steadfast character. Because of his modest lifestyle, skill, and experience, he had stood unfaltering against the pressures and blackmail of criminal circles and politics bearing the main weight of the harsh and challenging cases. Now, he was well-affirmed both as a person and a prosecutor. He was stripped of emotion or passion, competent and coldly level-headed in his decision-making. When he looked back and remembered the road he had traversed in life, it seemed as though the professional war he waged against crime and criminals, against those who try to snuff out the slightest hope of life, had been his mission, precisely like the bite into an apple in a smoke-saturated office. *So, it looks like a person remains a mystery and his own worst enemy,* Martin pondered, lost in thought. *Doesn't almost everything that happens to us originate from people? Who has killed more than man has killed man? How many people have died from the ravaging of wolves or dogs? How many human lives have been taken by snakes or bears? And man, how many of his ilk has he slain? When will we ever be saved from us?*

In front of him stood a caveman, a figment of his imagination. *Now, a sated and gratified man no longer needs to devour man, and so he merely kills and withdraws, throwing an indifferent glance over his shoulder at the rivulets of blood. We remain nothing but cave dwellers in modern times. This was yet another inner howl of Martin Guri.* No one was listening.

***

Only one day earlier, Martin had finalized the conclusions on one of the most volatile cases yet, which had shaken public opinion to the core. This was the case of charges brought against Marjan Boja, a name so often mentioned, a senior-ranking exponent of organized crime and one of the most dangerous criminals in the country. After almost one year of investigation, he felt relieved that he could finally seek closure. The day after tomorrow, Martin was to present his most notable indictment at Court. He was optimistic that with the evidence accumulated with his solidly convincing reasoning, the Court would find it imperative to pass a hefty sentence against the accused, Marjan Boja.

During all these months, the media had whipped up a frenzy of comments about how the mechanism worked which this criminal had used to commit such serious crimes. They dubbed him the *Drug Baron* or the *Super Killer*. The news broadcasts showed immeasurable exaggeration, misinformation, and super-scandalous editorial headlines. They had twisted themselves into knots over this case: unsolved murders, Mafia-like assassination attempts in the middle of the capital, and international drug trafficking. For weeks now, newspapers front-paged the arrested suspect under explosive headlines, and whether intentionally or otherwise, they had made him one of the most talked-about names in circulation.

Martin Guri never bought a newspaper at Tirana's many corner newspaper kiosks. He seldom watched the political analysts on television expounding on endless absurd theories in a desperate fight to secure ratings. It was quite a while now since he had distanced himself from the media outlets, several of which, in his opinion, had an expedient partnership with the criminal world and its bankrolling. In his house, no one followed televised chronicles or debates on crime, not only because they were harmful and distressing for the children but because, as Martin would say, "The only participants in these shows are the ones who are not worth giving the time of day to."

He had this constant feeling of malaise because not a day went by without the media cramming TV screens and newspapers with images of criminals, gang members, and prostitutes escorting them. *These worthless nonentities are transformed into heroes and super-models, and that is suicide for us. This is a return to cave-dwellers crime,* Martin Guri said. Quite often, when driving or alone in the office, he would let it out and shout, *"Enough! You are killing our young people. Enough!* It was not rare for him to wonder whether he should get himself invited to one of these studios and give it to them, face to face: *"You are the mouthpieces of crime! You should be the ones in the dock!!*

His mission was to wage war against crime, while those screen analysts are frequently sponsored by crime. *How the hell can we protect life? What must be done so that discourse is about life?!* He had given up waiting for an answer. He felt so lonely in these desperate appeals. At times of tension and stress, he would recall the words of his Literature teacher etched on his mind from his youth. "The world will not get better by complaining, but by doing your very best at what you do best... that will fix the world!" Martin had done that religiously daily but suddenly faced a conundrum he did not know how to solve. If only my Lit. teacher were still alive...He would have been the only person I could have unburdened myself to, and he would have given me the right advice. He was not a believer, so he would not go to his graveside to pray to him for advice. Martin Guri was cut from a different cloth. "Keep doing what you know best," his teacher's words came to him as if from lines of poetry. And he did exactly that in the turbulence that seemed to be steering him toward the cave.

That afternoon's meeting was nothing like the usual run of meetings before a case was brought to Court. It had been a dreadful nightmare. Marjan Boja, the criminal who awaited sentencing, kept cropping up in his mind's eye like an apparition.

He felt the tension and nervousness build up feverishly. He had experienced a host of situations where the adrenalin had hit the roof, danger lurking around every turn, the highs of triumph and success, the lows of failure, loss, and suspicion, but the psychological charge of this meeting was entirely different. This kind of anxiety was uncharted territory for him. He racked his brain for a decision, a way out, an escape from the swamp he had been sucked into, hook, line, and sinker. His troubled gaze dissolved into the night beyond, but he could feel the confusion mounting. Insecurity triggered panic.

He stood up from the armchair, returned to his desk, and confronted his computer screen. The urge was to write something. He soon discarded the idea. He simply couldn't write a thing; nothing came to him. Picking up the file of charges against Marjan Boja, which was printed that morning and left on his desk, he leafed through it. A multitude of pages, all neatly stacked and numbered, entire episodes of offenses committed by the accused. The mechanism of events, the evidence, the arguments supporting the charges brought, the legal analysis, and everything else were all laid out here. Everything is described down to the most minute detail. Murder, drug trafficking, assassinations. These pages comprised the entire grim criminal situation that prevailed nationwide. The episodes of crimes recorded there were common occurrences in his country. Most of them were unsolved. Martin had read and edited the material several times. He had reread the whole file diagonally to reassure himself that the extent of Marjan Bojas's crimes was complete. He wasn't lucid enough to correct anything, even if he had wanted to. His professional way of reasoning was exhausted.

He felt shattered. He was on the verge of capitulation. At that moment in time, the crimes committed by Marjan Bojan seemed somehow lighter than the deadweight pressing down on his chest. He thought about opening the black safe embedded in the wall, precisely to the left of the armchair where he was sitting.

Stashed away in this steel safe were the most secret components of his dossiers: transcribed text of phone conversations between individuals of enormous power and influence, top-secret documents that were for his eyes only, photographs and surveillance videos linked to highly volatile cases, his service sidearm, which he rarely carried, and his father's old wristwatch, a favourite keepsake.

He remembered that he had better call his wife Eliza to say he would be late. He hesitated. The prosecutor's Code is no phone calls. He always returned home, and she was always there, smiling and waiting for him, irrespective of the hour. Eliza's eyes never lied to him or their children.

Sitting there in solitude, he had no idea how long this night would be—it could be the longest night of his life. He felt as if he was physically going grey because of the darkness invading his soul. He recalled that woman's words, which had toppled his world and planted deep anguish in his heart and soul.

"Do it for me, Martin! He is all I live for; do it, please!"

Her words had cleaved deeply into his chest like a venom-tipped dagger. He had looked into eyes, those strange eyes. He had never experienced an imposition of this nature. It was as if that curt, abrupt tone of her voice that followed the tears dissolved in the radiance of the ring she wore with its very costly diamonds. Speaking with a kind of delicate softness, she had said, "Do it before I speak with you again, but I will not be speaking to you as I am now! But do it for your own sake as well!"

She had pulled the door to as she left, and it had clicked shut gently. To him, that click had resounded like the clunk of the coffin's lid being lifted into place.

"Do it before I speak to you again, but not like this!"

These words rattled around inside his head, echoing so powerfully. They shocked the hell out of him. Nothing he had been through remotely resembled the hurricane Arjana had created. She hadn't brought any information that could influence the closing statement, nothing but the blinding brilliance of the diamond ring. An inner weariness washed through him. He was exhausted. A cold sweat broke out all over his body. He felt the energy drain from him. He poured himself yet another glass of whisky. It was freezing outside, but within him, a volcano blazed. Like a huge, heaving crater, it was as if his chest was ready to erupt, scorching the earth and everything he had built over all these years.

How had he never understood that he had been the happiest of men until this meeting? Now and then, something happened, even a mere conversation, that sent shock waves deep into your world. Returning to what used to hold meaning for you becomes an impossible mission.

Chapter II
Triptych of memories

Gutted, he summoned what strength and willpower he could muster (like trying to revive post-Waterloo foot soldiers) and headed home. He could not sit in that oppressive smoke-filled office until the morning. He was almost suffocating, and apart from that, the apparition of Arjana had begun to weave in and out of the smoke vapours surrounding him.

As always, Eliza was waiting for him, the trappings of dinner neatly arranged on the table. They ate breakfast together at this table, too. The oversized dining table in the sitting room was only set when they had guests. Eliza never fully understood Martin's situation because he was always exhausted when he came home. Even when he was in a good mood, a phone call was enough to derail everything.

However, despite this, Martin devoted all weekends and holidays to his family, with the rare exception. His dedication to holidays was genuine; he needed to shrug off the mantel of prosecutor so he could come alive as a down-to-earth, regular family man.

Until this afternoon, when Arjana turned up at his office, Martin had stood his ground on his terms, withstanding all the attacks, provocations, hardships, and challenges. Other cases had brought him face to face with serious criminal offenses, but he had had the law on his side and had kept his sights unerringly focused on it. Only this time, his family was involved. Its very foundations and his relationship with Eliza were under threat. What Arjana had done was throw a noose around Martin Guri's family bliss, and there was every chance that she could tighten this stranglehold until his last breath.

As he sat eating dinner (not hungry at all), he glanced furtively at Eliza. She did her best to get Martin to chill and relax, talking softly about her and the children's day, relating episodes from life around them, and gently petting him as she headed for the fruit bowl or a glass of water from the kitchen.

Eliza flittered around him like a moth attracted to a light bulb, and Martin agonized over the fear that she could be electrocuted and collapse to the ground.

He watched her as he had never done before, but still, he could not bring himself to say a word. He wanted to shelter her within his fist and close his fingers tightly around her, where not only Arjana but even the devil himself wouldn't find her. He thought of the many years he had journeyed to reach what he had with Eliza today, a happiness he did not want to forfeit for anything.

…It had been a routine day at work when Artur Rasa had said to him, "Love is like a bolt of lightning; it doesn't hit the same spot twice! Eliza seems amazing; she is your fate written in the stars just for you; you have got to believe that!"

Immersed in his world of piles of papers, files, and offices, Artur's advice had been like a rap on the door deep within Martin's heart. Sitting at one of the local bars, chatting over a beer, Artur had been adamant, "Don't throw away this opportunity, Martin. Life is not just work; you're also a person, flesh and bone, like everyone else. I know you'll remember me on this one. You don't need to say a word. I saw it in how you looked at each other; I noticed that something had shifted." There had been numerous occasions when Artur had spoken to Martin about different girls, but never with such intensity and seriousness as he did when referring to Eliza. Martin veiled his emotions, but in the end, he gave in, admitting his feelings for her and that this had become a real torture for him. "You know, you are one of the few who can read me, Turi," Martin had said to him, "and this time, you guessed right." They had both laughed heartily with the sheer joy of Martin's promise of happiness. As far as Martin was concerned, Eliza was the woman he had dreamed of for years. Deep down, he had always believed such a woman would someday enter his life.

He married Eliza when she worked for the Judicial Police. Freshly graduated from the Faculty of Literature, she was hired as a media spokesperson for the institution Martin had just been appointed the head of. After their marriage, Eliza chose to devote herself to teaching, electing not to work in the same place as her husband.

He recalled it as if it were today when he first saw Eliza. He had been mesmerized by this girl brimming with laughter. Her eyes shone so brightly that it seemed they lit up the darkness. They were such intelligent eyes, full of life. He had felt a burning sensation in his chest, resembling "the sting of a bee," Martin often recalled. Gradually, the effect of the "bee venom" had spread through his chest, numbing his heart. He realized this one day when he thought he could feel the blood pounding through his veins. Instinctively, he placed his hand on his chest, trying to fathom the tingle that radiated from his heart and permeated his whole body. The effect amplified particularly if he pictured her in his mind or if she were close to his office, talking to his colleagues about the official announcements of the day. In a word, he had understood and believed that his love for Eliza was real. As a person of fortified self-control, he had no idea how to harness the power of the volcano that had erupted in his chest and was suffocating him. Everything had to be done discreetly to avoid the risk of their attachment being endangered before it had a chance to thrive. The care he took and the maturity he demonstrated were evidence that this love had indeed been conceived.

At first glance, Eliza seemed to effortlessly take things in her stride and discharge commitments just as easily. She gave Martin the impression that they had known each other for a long time, although it had only been a few days. She laughed freely and heartily at the witticisms they exchanged like an old friend familiar with his ways. She also liked Martin exactly how he was: withdrawn and severe but straightforward to talk to, compassionate, and proper.

When it came to "managing this romantic volcano," it was apparent that Martin didn't have much experience. Although he tried hard to prevent Eliza from picking up on this fact, it was an impossible mission from the outset. He was in a perpetual state of bewilderment, nervousness, numbness, alarm, and confusion. He went through these emotional upheavals at home, but also at work, in the office, or walking down the street, to the point where he began to think of himself as a "patient" with a heart complaint.

- Could Eliza be stringing me along? - He did wonder sometimes because she was so open, a genuine free spirit who found conversation with him a walk in the park. He never plucked up the courage to impose limits. Then he would think that she didn't even want to know about the feelings that were torturing him. His inability to penetrate her emotions annoyed him. The more vulnerable he felt in her presence, the more she upped the dosages of refusal and mystery, exhausting him. He went as far as rationalizing things with wariness and mistrust: *It could be that she is trying to butter up to the boss, as girls without character, incompetent and insecure do to secure their jobs, ready to sacrifice everything, including sentiments and dignity.*

He was waging a battle with himself, which is why his prejudices enveloped Eliza, too, who was not at all one of those girls without character that Martin suspected. His irrationality stopped him from breaking the ice to speak openly with Eliza. *"I'm nothing but a classic wimp when it comes to these matters,"* he repeatedly said to himself while struggling to gain control of these complicated situations, which were nothing other than love.

All the dread he felt lurked in a sentence like, "Thank you, I feel very flattered, I hold you in high regard but only as a colleague. I have no feelings for you like that," which Eliza may have on the tip of her tongue. The fear that something like that could happen held Martin in check, paralyzed. He could not cross that threshold. As far as her conduct went, Eliza reflected nothing but maximum correctness and excellent manners in communicating with the officials. However, in Martin's case, the energy felt different, especially toward the end of the day, when the job was done and everyone felt more relaxed. These were the vibes that carried the thrill of her provocations and which wrenched at his heart. This was the point of departure, and he had to embark yesterday on his quest to win this woman. In his soul, he felt something unique happened when he came up against her. It was an inexplicable awkwardness, turmoil, and pull, but not simply the instinct of a male attracted to a gorgeous woman, and there was no doubt that Eliza was undoubtedly that. This was not something casual. Day by day, Eliza would permeate his very being as a man until she completely overtook it.

***

"Tell Eliza I would like to see her in my office, please," Martin asked of the employee from the Human Resources Office, who was always carrying files under her arm whenever she came to his office. Her job was to update the employees' files and manage the day-to-day correspondence.

After a few minutes, Eliza walked into his office without knocking. She stood there in front of him, not saying a word.

He took his time as he looked at her…Interesting. How could he not realize how much he missed her? All he wanted to do was to put his strong arms around her and kiss her passionately, but all he managed was to mumble vaguely.

"You never knock before entering an office, it seems?" His face did not reflect this half reproach half quip as he forced himself to look as serious as he could.

Unprepared and entirely taken by surprise by Martin's reaction, Eliza felt her face go red with embarrassment. She whispered incoherently, and her body shook like an autumn leaf in the wind.

"Forgive me, I didn't mean to; I don't know what I was thinking…"

She then stood and waited for the directions or orders she had been summoned for. She followed the news very closely as it broke during the day, all press statements and comments connected to all the aspects of the work of this institution. She did excellent work in thoroughly compiling and seeking consultation on all messages released to the public as the official mouthpiece of the Judicial Police. She never had time to go out for coffee during office hours. The intensification of the job dynamics had ended free coffee breaks during working hours for everybody. The coffee shops and bars in the vicinity of the institution were seeing less and less business during working hours.

"Please write up a draft for me by tomorrow on the developments of the month, main events, and the winding up of investigations on closed cases." Martin lifted his head from the files on his desk and continued looking her straight in the eye.

"I am concerned about the volatile rantings of certain media analysts; they are completely at sea when they talk about our work. I read your summary of media comments. They are now discussing real cases, divulging details, and making highly sensitive references that harm our investigations. Please think about the sensitive issues they hone in on and statements we should send them as information. We must ensure that what they get is what we want to give them in the interests of the public, our investigations, and our war against crime. Media advertisement campaigns of political analysts are the last thing we need. They're the ones who need the news from us. So, I would like you to write up a draft where we come across accurately and directly, but without revealing details that damage our work." After delivering these guidelines, he lowered his eyes to the papers before him, indicating he had nothing more to say and that she should go.

Eliza stood in the middle of the office as if rooted to the spot. She jotted down something in her notebook. She didn't utter a word. She nodded as if saying a very disjointed "goodbye," turned on her heel, and walked out of the office. She felt the tears well up. Martin's words reverberated in her head: *Don't you ever knock, Miss...before entering someone's office. Never? You, Miss...A material... By tomorrow... Awareness... sensitive... details... accurate.*

Irrespective of the more frequent conversations and furtive touching, which aroused them even more, it was quite a while until one weekend, Martin plucked up the courage to ask Eliza to meet him after work. They met close to the National Library, where books are sold in the corner kiosks and on the street, CDs are sold in the little side stalls, and live music is played on the street, where prayers offered up to God ricochet gently off the walls of one of Tirana's oldest mosques...in short, a memorable spot.

This was the first time they met outside the workplace, just the two of them.

"It is such a beautiful city, Tirana; I love it here. It is like some enormous house where I grew up, even though it has altered so much, and I can hardly find traces of Tirana of yore. What about you, Eliza? How do you feel in this city?" he asked, striving to read the answer in her eyes.

"Tirana is just as beautiful to me, too, but you know us, from Shkodra, we love Shkodra more. Every time I return to Shkodra, I understand how closely I am tied to it. I think hometowns, where we are born, are like mothers, and although we leave them, no other lap compares to laying our heads on, so to say, no matter how luxurious it may be. Fortunately, I would say, Shkodra has not undergone the transformation Tirana has, which is fast becoming a metropolis."

"Believe me," she said, losing her Shkodra accent as if she had just returned to Tirana. I think it is irrational to relocate to Tirana just to be an inhabitant of the metropolis. A person has two lives: one with others and another with themself. In my case, both these existences are inextricably linked with my hometown. Separating them is tantamount to betrayal."

When Eliza spoke, her accent and dialect melody touched Martin even more. He only wanted to hear her talk without stopping; it was like listening to a concert of Shkodra jare folk songs, which he loved listening to while driving. Conversation flowed freely, and she readily agreed to continue driving for a while longer.

Being close to her, his mind was not really on the conversation or where he was going. He felt transfixed, unsure, dizzy, suspended somewhere between Earth and Heaven, the air and fragments of the soul, between reality and Dreamworld. Without realizing it, they had driven quite a distance. They were both lost in meditation. They seldom broke the silence with questions and answers about targeted subjects and had put quite a distance between Tirana and themselves.

From the top of the Castle of Rozafa, Shkodra stretched out below, shrouded in a mystic beauty. They took it all in, gazing at the city below them. It seemed to be floating in the waters of its lake and rivers, its street lights softly illuminating every nook and cranny, a breathtaking shimmer as dusk drew the day to a close. Eliza stood in stunned silence. She was in the city she loved with all her heart. Martin was just as spellbound. He gazed down at the city, encircled by its lake, rivers, and distant, towering mountains.

"Do you know what, Martin…" Eliza began to say, but her voice trailed off. *I can't believe I am standing here with you, in my hometown, in Rozafa Castle. I had never imagined I could be here with you. Here with you?! I feel I am dreaming!"*

Gradually, lovingly, she relaxed into another person, tender and sentimental, laying bare all the pent-up feelings and emotions locked away deep in her heart for so long. They had had feelings for each other for a long time, but, like Martin, Eliza had also been reserved. However, this had not been an indication of refusal. This was her shield against the powerful feelings she nurtured for Martin, her boss. And now, here she was, with him, in Rozafa Castle, in her hometown. It was like being in a dream. Eliza, you know full well how significant this moment is, tread carefully, she said to herself.

He murmured, "Well, wake up Liza. We're here, just the two of us…"

Martin reached out shyly at first, and his hand brushed against hers. She didn't draw her hand away. She didn't budge an inch. She held his gaze steadily, her eyes overflowing with exultation that lit up her whole face. It was as if she had been waiting so long for this moment. They could wait no longer. Their lips met in a long and passionate kiss without understanding how exactly, both yearning to quell the flames of intense passion that consumed them. It was as though they had been purposely made for each other, with all their hopes and dreams, their dreams of today and their tomorrows, with the warm, sunny days, but also with the cloudy days, with the seasons and the elements.

Dusk had long since fallen. It was late. Just the two of them, alone, in that corner of the ruins of Rozafa Castle, the day surrendering to the impinging darkness of night, was like a mirage. It felt as though the Castle had been overwhelmed by them, whereas they had been overwhelmed by each other.

"Martin, I wouldn't wish the fate of Rozafa on anyone."

"It's just a legend, a myth, a ballad! Why on earth would you suffer a fate like that?"

"Your job, Martin, your duty, everything… It is all an immense sacrifice. But, if you ever need me, I will be there for you. I love you so much, Martin Guri!" she whispered, nestled in his embrace.

"That's love talking, but you're right. When you love someone, you naturally fear for them and yourself, like I do for you." This was his way of avowing that he loved her just as much. Silence descended. They remained like that for a long while, in each other's arms, aroused as they touched and felt the heat of their breathing.

"Eliza, I have waited for this day my whole life, perhaps even before I knew you."

Even though Martin tried hard to persuade her to stay the night in Shkodra, Eliza insisted they return to Tirana.

"What's happening tomorrow?"

"Tomorrow is Sunday," she said, smiling.

"Will we be together forever?" Martin asked before they departed. Eliza, still snuggled up against him, nodded, answering with eyes that shone with happiness.

This is my Martin, she said to herself, her mind and heart still a little bashful, and her silence spoke reams; love was in her heart to stay. This was her first love, and her heart, mind, body, and lips were on fire.

It began to drizzle just after midnight, light and gentle but persistent. The whole world was engulfed in tranquillity. To them, the sound of the droplets drumming against the car's windscreen was like the most amazing symphony they had ever experienced.

"Eliza, I wonder if you realize that you have the power to make me your slave for life; you have mesmerized me."

"Do you regret that?" she asked with child-like innocence.

His head drooped as *if slightly hurt*, but he didn't reply. Should he tell her?! But then, what would he tell her?! *What a complete idiot! When has the virginity of a male ever come up for discussion? No such claim has ever been made, not even amongst the "Burrënesha" (Sworn virgins). Forget about it! The man was born to dominate the woman!*

Standing on the footpath, she paused before walking off towards her home. She reached up and whispered in his ear:

"Forgive me, I'm not like you! I...," she stammered, her eyes brimming with tears... "Eliza, you are my love and my life!"

"Oh, dear God, Martin, if you only knew how much I have longed for this moment. You are my life and my love, too. We are both each other's love and life, Martin!"

Their parting kiss seemed to last for eternity. The sweet taste of that kiss lingered with him that night, rocking to the rhythm of the soothing rain, together with his soul and entire being.

That evening was to remain forever the happiest of his entire life.

***

It had been a long time since Martin Guri had brought the memories of his love story with Eliza to mind. So, it had taken Arjana's mysterious knock on the door for him to recall and weigh up all the spiritual wealth that cocooned him and, even more importantly, the risk of losing it.

"Eli, I'll be in my studio for a little while. I want to look over a couple of things. Don't wait up for me, go to bed, it may take a little longer...If I fall asleep, I'll sleep on the sofa in there...don't worry," he said to Eliza, who was almost asleep on her feet.

"All right, sweetheart. It's up to you but be careful not to fall off to sleep without throwing something around your shoulders. I don't want you getting a cold," his wife replied with her usual concern.

Martin changed into the clothes he wore around the house, comfortable loungewear that also kept him warm. Although

Spring was just around the corner, nights were beautiful and crisp in Tirana.

Martin's studio was like an annex of his office at work. It was here that he would finish off most of the day's work, during the long nights, in silence, in the bosom of his family, so close and yet so far away. Silence and peace remained one of the keys to the successful processing of investigation cases. There were always interruptions at work: day-to-day, routine administrative work unrelated to the files of investigations, relations with institutions that sought replies, the comings and goings of colleagues, and endless other commitments. This killed any chance of focusing on given details, which essentially often constituted the turning point in delicate processes.

He flipped the switch on one of the softer lights in the studio and looked over at the armchair where he had a habit of sitting before picking up a case file. He half-filled a glass with "Jägermeister" and settled back into the armchair, his gaze wandering around his studio. Apart from the small shelves of vocational publications in Albanian and foreign languages, several paintings adorned the walls, most of them gifted by friends on special occasions. One was a tableau depicting a scene from northern Albania, a village where his family used to go for summer holidays when he was a child. This is where his father was born. He often found himself recounting stories to colleagues, friends, or even Eliza, from those happy times embedded in his memory, despite the circumstances of a dictatorship and extreme poverty. He was surrounded by the love, affection, and care of the people there, and this was Martin's treasure back then, but even in later years, as he grew to manhood.

This whole thing that had taken place in the office with Arjana was like the trajectory of a bulldozer careening toward him. He felt utterly deserted in the face of an oncoming tempest, deluge, avalanche, evil!

That painting on the wall, coupled with his dismal state of mind, whisked him back, as if a film was being rewound, to a tragic event of many years ago. It was during the school holidays when he witnessed the drowning of a young man in the river that ran past the village. Even though dozens of villagers joined hands to form a barrier across the waters, they failed to save him. All they managed to do was drag the lifeless form up onto the bank. Who could he count on to be there, to form a barrier to save him from the onslaught of evil that was Arjana? He withdrew into the memories of what occurred so many years ago in the waters of the river of his remote village, a tragedy that moved everyone immeasurably.

…It was summer, unbearable heat like the days of August are. A beautiful river meandered along the valley floor, cleaving the mountain range in two. The bare rock faces of the mountains sizzled in the scorching heat. Martin's wise old grandmother used to say, "You can bake bread in the sun." That's how hot it got. That Saturday in the middle of August, for some reason, he had felt a kind of inner alarm, as if the stone and the wood generated heat. As far as the eye could see, everything in the sky and on the ground, even the pores in peoples' skin, perspired agonizingly. It was utterly out of the question to stay in the sun. You had to find some shade or walk beneath the canopy of the trees, refresh yourself at a spring, and avoid going backward and forward outside, especially around midday.

Without warning, the sky darkened. First, clouds appeared scurrying about the peaks in the mountain range in the western reaches of the Valley, over "Pidgeon Peaks," as they were called. Then, they began scampering along at a great pace, pushing one another eastward, simultaneously releasing distant peals of thunder and faint, pale flashes. They were bearing down on the village with a purpose, and the day dimmed in a matter of minutes. The earth and the air blackened. The peals of thunder and the crackle of lightning were everywhere and very close, rumbling overhead, above the roof, electrifying the tops of oak and willow trees, rattling windowpanes, scouring the riverbanks, prying into the cooperative's livestock stalls and making the bushes in the backyard of the house where Martin was staying, tremble and shiver. A blanket of darkness had settled over everything as if dusk had fallen. Martin had ensconced himself on the windowsill. He fiddled with the window, opening and closing it. Beside him were the reading books his Literature teacher had given him to get through over the summer break. He gazed lovingly at the picturesque view stretching down to the river's bank. His cousins, who lived in that house, all slept together in a smaller room next to the living room, reserved for guests. This room echoed the booms of the storm, too. The howling wind that ushered in the storm roared even louder. Some of the towering branches on the willow trees, about twenty meters from the house, torn away from the trunk, snapped like a bird's wing. This was all happening under the dominance of the thunderstorm, a gale out of nowhere as it muscled its way on. The first drops of rain forewarned the deluge.

It thrilled Martin to watch the trees creak and bend just like the weeping willow branches surrender to the river's flow without the slightest defiance or resistance. He wanted to watch the roof tiles fly off into the storm, the abnormal howling of the dogs, the terrified bleating of the sheep and goats, and the muffled braying of the donkey in the stall about fifty meters from the house. He watched the villagers hurrying home to slam their doors on the gale or run for temporary cover until the worst had passed. He watched as another neighbour impatiently coaxed a few livestock into safe shelters.

At moments like these, Martin longed to open the window to feel to the very core, the music, the play, the waltz Mother Nature whirled around to. Granny Florija scolded him, warning him against catching a cold. But, to little avail, the urge within him grew stronger and deeper; Mother Nature mesmerized him, lured and completely absorbed him. Granny Florija's advice, sadly, went in one ear and out the other.

And then the rainstorm was on them. It hit with a deafening uproar. He couldn't recall anything like it. Martin thought, how could the earth withstand the ear-splitting thunderclaps and such fearsome lightning bolts? The soil emitted a dry, pungent smell, and like a tinder-dry sponge, it sucked up the rain that had hit it with such fury. His granny muttered a prayer under her breath, closing it with a louder pronounced, "Please save us, dear God." My uncle and Granny Florija retreated into the kitchen. The door slammed shut, more because of the draughts caused by the raging storm than my uncle's haste. They had secured their few goats and sheep and had driven home all the bolts on the doors and windows. "Martin, get yourself into the kitchen; that's quite enough of this fiddling with the window; open, close, open, close," my uncle scolded me. He made sure we were all present, safe and sound, inside.

"Here, take these, put these extra shirts on," Granny Florida persisted, holding out a long-sleeved, flannel shirt to each of us. "You catch cold easier in the summer than in the winter!" Granny's mutterings now resounded in that tiny room of the house, "God, save us!"

Even in the kitchen, Martin made a space for himself in front of the window, completely absorbed and fascinated with what was happening outside. No longer was the water dripping off the awnings of the tiled roofs, but it was gushing off like small, accumulating streams, drumming down onto the small backyard area.

My uncle, with a jacket slung over his shoulders, ventured into the backyard for a second time and headed for the stall with the livestock. Granny Florija lit the kerosene lamp. There was an inky darkness. One after the other, flashes of lightning illuminated the room with their ghostly light. Martin was the only one who could hardly wait for the next lightning bolt, fearless, feeling light as a feather, as if he had long awaited this moment. He relished the show put on by such weather so much: the powerlessness of the willows, the oak trees, the trails, the cobbles, the barn, the lean-tos; the fragility of the pots of flowers Granny Florija lined up on both sides of the yard, the leaves on the trees, whirling and swaying in the eye of the storm, the miniature rivulets that gurgled and gushed wherever formed; the confusion and chaos at the offices of the cooperative, the havoc wrecked high up on the mountain slopes and peaks. Nothing could withstand the force of Nature. Only in the face of this blind fury did people bow their heads and remember that they should offer up a prayer as a final wish to a place somewhere above that ominous blackened sky, a place where humility counted, somewhere, high above. In those times, praying and seeking God's forgiveness were prohibited; there was only "belief in the Party." My wise old Granny continued doing her own thing, "We must seek God's pardon every day and not just when it's terrible weather outside. Too late. Now, wait for the lightning bolts from Him, up in Heaven," she said. She prayed the way she knew how; every day, it was her ritual. Martin often tried to imitate her, but listening to her devise her prayers, he often found them funny, and he would rush out of the room, slam the door, and collapse in giggles. "You little scoundrel, how dare you laugh at my prayers," she would shout, but Martin was already scampering out of the yard. They were all memories now.

He had no idea how much time had elapsed when the storm began to wane. Calm descended as the railway tracks creaked in relief with the passing of the final train carriage. It had been one, maybe two hours, but he remembered that with the weakening of the storm when the sky began to peep through again, he took to his heels and ran straight down to the river, as it was his habit.

- Granny's prayers did save us, - Martin said to himself, drawing nearer to a bunch of villagers who were fast gathering like the clouds before the storm. He was dying to find out more from the gathering.

When he arrived, he saw that dozens of villagers, men, women, and children had rallied on both river banks. Never had he seen that usually small flow of water so swollen in the middle of summer. Probably, not even the village old folk could remember a summer when the river's waters had risen like this. The water surged downstream, dark and murky. It arched its back like an incensed dark brown bull itching to charge and sweep away everything in its path. You could see branches and trunks of trees brought down from the mountains bobbing up and down furiously as the current swept them on. Then he heard voices saying, "Oh, how sad, what a shame!" So many onlookers, to the side of me, nearby, everywhere! The carcasses of drowned sheep and goats hurtled downstream in the foam of the waves. In the chaos of that moment, someone howled out with such a sense of calamity that everyone turned as if by command.

"What, what is it? Has someone fallen into the water?!"

"Someone is drowning; they're drowning!" voices repeated in confusion.

"The river is carrying him down in our direction, toward us, here!" a man shouted.

"A man, a woman, or a child?!

Martin froze. He was slightly built, so he squeezed himself into a corner and stood there staring, taking everything in. If the truth were known, everyone was a little dumbfounded, and as if by command, again, all the onlookers moved as one downstream to a spot where the riverbed widened. Here, the turbulence of the water calmed down a little as the river took a deep breath before rushing on. Martin ran downstream with the rest of them. His heart was beating differently. He could feel the beats as if his heart were ready to burst out of his chest. *I don't get it! Granny prayed for everyone in the village, so why did this happen? Why was her prayer not heard?*

The villagers lined up, forming a living dam.

Two, three, five, he lost count of the number of youths and men, hands firmly clasped, wading into the water. Holding on to one another for dear life, they were edging out from the bank to face the barrage of water coming straight at them.

"Watch out for the tree trunks!" one of them shouted out.

"Watch out for the rolling boulders," cried another.

"Watch, you don't slip! Side on, side on to the current! Hang on tight to one another!"

One man in the middle of the line shouted the most. He must have been strong and experienced in such situations. Within minutes, the people lining both banks had almost doubled. In shock, they followed the people in the water, fighting to withstand its impact. They were all tense and stood there waiting, agog with anxiety.

"We can see him, he's coming!" someone yelled.

"Steady now, tighten up!"

"Sideways to the current!" boomed the man's voice in the middle of the river.

This was Sabri, the P.E. teacher at the village school. He was leading the rescue effort. All the others followed his command. A human barricade had been formed, waiting to receive the body of goodness knows who. Martin managed to detect the moment when the body careened into and came to rest against the human barricade. He would have given the world to be in the water with the others, just like a real hero, or at least like a person who resisted on that disastrous day, as most villagers described it.

It was the body of a young man in his early twenties who, as we found out later, lived in one of the remote villages of the neighbouring cooperative. He had been guarding the cooperative's goat herds when the devastating storm had erupted. No one knew for certain, but they said he probably slipped or had jumped into the river to save the livestock.

"What does it matter at the end of the day," the P.E. teacher said, his dripping clothes clinging to him, "The poor man drowned..." Sabri said bringing the subject to a close.

"So young, he departed from this life before he had time to enjoy it," someone else added sadly. One of the onlookers on the riverbank recognized the victim. The adults and the elders decided to take the body of the young man back to his village in the cooperative's vehicle. Cleaning up and preparing the body according to custom took a while. Martin heard that the next day, practically the whole zone had turned up at the funeral, including the district's senior Party and Local Government members. Martin gleaned from the conversations at home that the First Secretary of the Party Committee had promised the dedicated shepherd, Hajri Kacani (this was the name of the victim), was to be proclaimed a Hero of Socialist Labour, for the self-sacrificing heroism he displayed in safeguarding common property.

Later, songs were sung to him, but he was never decorated as "Hero of Socialist Labour." Apparently, there were issues with his family biography. His uncle had done several years in prison charged with "propaganda against the people's power", so individuals with such blemishes on their family records could never be proclaimed heroes! Poor old Hajri, such bad luck, both alive and deceased.

***

And now, Martin is treading very frightening currents himself, not visible ones, like the river torrents, but all the same, his legs trembled uncontrollably as they flailed, searching for the bottom. Could he become a victim of a flash flood, too? That's exactly how Arjana swept into his office. Like a summer storm, she mercilessly unleashed the elements against him. What about the prosecutor? Would he fall a "martyr" with a blemished record, like the young man,

Hajri Kacani, whose uncle was a declared enemy of the Party?!

"Enemy of the Party!" It had been ages since he had heard these tragic, comical words spoken out loud. The full title used to be "Enemy of the Party and the People." He grimaced, trying to recall an "Enemy of the Party and the People" he had known.

When he was a child, he had no understanding of what the duties of a prosecutor could be, and very little or no mention was made at school about these functions. To be condemned as an "enemy of the party and people" was like being branded with a searing white-hot iron, marked for life, like the brands burnt into the skin of slaves of Roman times. This branding followed you for life, even after serving a sentence. This was the imprint on your back and the "blemish" in the personal records of your entire family.

When he was younger, Martin had often asked himself: *Why is it not simply "Enemy of the People?" Wasn't the party a part of the people? Was the party not made up of the people? Why was this distinct and counter-opposing word group sometimes required?*

He had asked his father one day, with the inhibition and hesitation of a teenager, "If you're declared an enemy of the people, aren't you automatically an enemy of the party too? Why do they always say, "enemy of the party and people," and not simply, "enemy of the people?" His father, perturbed by the question his son asked, thought that perhaps someone had tried to provoke his son. So, his reply was abrupt and curt, "The Party is at the helm, and the people follow on behind." Martin had got the message - his parents were very careful with such conversations. Martin often heard the expression used at home, "Even the walls have ears!" He had been quite surprised the first time he heard it, and his gaze had traveled over the walls of the house as if trying to locate "the ears" which he never found; this was one of the enigmatic expressions of his parents until he grew up and got the gist of things…

Ensconced comfortably in his office armchair, his mind wandering back and forth down memory lane, Martin recalled when he had seen a prosecutor for the very first time. Back then, he had no idea what a prosecutor was and what the position represented, and even less so imagined that he might become one.

There was this dramatic story of the poor cart driver, Rushan…

It was rumored that Rushan, the cart driver, had a whole cartload of children born into this world, one after the other at the end of each year for eight years on end. He worked extremely hard; he was always working, but it was claimed that he was somewhat light-fingered; in other words, he misappropriated things. Every evening, he would rein in the horse and cart outside his home, located on the edge of the village, apart from the rest of the houses. He unloaded his "loot" of the day, and then he would head off for the center of the cooperative. There, he unloaded the occasional bag of flour, or a basket of bread, maize or wheat… "Rushan is so resourceful," the villagers would say, "he could draw food from a stone, that one!" This is what was said about him. In his eyes, those of a child, Martin believed Rushan, the cart driver, was far more honest and honourable than he needed to be. The malicious gossipers, the spiteful and lazy good-for-nothing villagers, were on his case all day, every day. Martin never believed, even today, that Rushan could steal things from his daily carting jobs for the cooperative, whether from the bakery, the village shop, the simple creamery, or the field crops as was claimed.

Disaster occurred one day, a catastrophe that would live on in the village's collective memory for a long time. Martin often recalled that summer day, and in detail, too. That day, the whole village was harvesting the wheat crops in the fields, bent over earnestly and slogging away at the day's tasks. Martin was at his uncle's house, where he spent his summer holidays. He knew everyone because he became the village's most inquisitive inhabitant during the summer of every year. His father had brought him up to say, "I am from Luginasi" (where his father was born) whenever he was asked where he came from, even though Martin had been born in Tirana.

Martin was walking along the road that led directly past Rushan's house and onto the other village neighbourhood across the river. From a distance, he could make out a stationary vehicle with all its doors ajar. It looked as though the driver was adjusting the vehicle's side mirror. A feeling of apprehension took hold of him. This was not just any vehicle; this jeep belonged to the local branch of the Internal Affairs office! Everyone knew it and feared it. After a little while, it moved on toward Rushan's house. Two police officers got out, then a third man dressed in a black suit. Martin recognized him. He was the local Internal Affairs officer for the zone. Piro, his name was. He hailed from a city in the south of the country, and to the locals, he was a total mystery. You rarely saw him with police backup when he came to the village. Except for the zone's Chief of Police, sometimes you would run into him in the company of the man in charge of the warehouse that came under the Section of Trade or with the Cooperative's Chief of Finance, also from the south. Whenever Martin saw the Chief of Finance, stubby, slightly bent over, and with a small pop-belly, he thought and still thinks to this day that all male Finance Chiefs are short, stout, but orderly, of few words, but still, mysterious.

The ordinary villagers avoided Piro. It was as if they feared him. It was as if he hailed from some human wasteland where people made from molten iron worked and lived; people poured without any particular life form, limbs, or senses. And it was the Internal Affairs Officer, Piro, who gave the orders as if by telecommand in this shapeless human wasteland - the narrow yard of Rushan's house. He was accompanied by two police officers and the ominous jeep of the Internal Affairs branch.

Martin froze. His mind went blank. Not a muscle moved. It was obvious that the Internal Affairs Officer and the police were not on a courtesy call. Something had happened in this village that nestled into one end of the valley, like a little ammonite fossil embedded in the rock. Very rarely did anything happen here outside of the ordinary, depleting monotony of unremarkable seasons. Perhaps Rushan had been caught with his hand in the cookie jar, as it was whispered in the village that he was light-fingered because of all the mouths he had to feed. The whole village had found out that two or three nights earlier, Rushan, the cart driver, had drunk himself into a stupor at the club in the middle of the village.

"I'm at my wit's end, so I drink." Rushan had said. "I drink because of my poor little girl who will grow up disabled, locked away indoors, pale, and never a smile on her lips. I can't bring myself to go home, especially this evening, because she turns eight today, but she has never crossed the threshold of the school. I drink because it would be better if I were struck down by lightning and burnt to a cinder. It pains me so much. I've been told that there is no cure for my little girl. She has this very rare disease that doesn't let her bones grow. Of all the people in the world, why my little girl? How did she get it?! But honestly, I would not wish this illness on anyone, not even my worst enemy. I suppose all illnesses are bad, and that's why they're called illnesses, but my little girl's illness has never been seen or heard of before. They told me that her only chance is to seek help abroad. But "abroad" is only an option for the big guns of this world, for those who live in Tirana, for the secretaries and the chairpersons, for who knows who! For people like us, poor people who do back-breaking work and have lost any hope, for the daughter of a cart driver, there is no "abroad," poor old Rushan mumbled to himself, lamenting his situation. The alcohol had gotten the better of him, and it seemed as if no one was listening to him anyway. He drowned his sorrows in the raki bottle.

"Rushan, I would be careful about what I said if I were you. You are letting your mouth run amok," said the coffee shop waiter.

"I don't give a shit what my mouth does. I am the world's most dim-witted peabrain," Rushan ranted in despair.

"I'm the crippled one, not my little girl. She's been condemned by God, along with me, but man has condemned all the rest of us. A man I call my brother, who has the same blood as I do, who I trust and who trusts me."

"Rushan, you have drunk enough. You won't find the solution in the bottom of a glass or a cure for your little daughter's illness," said the waiter, continuing his conversation.

"For your information, Avzi," Rushan said to the waiter (a distant cousin), "I took my little girl all the way to Tirana. You can't imagine what I went through. Eight hours on a bus! I carried my daughter on my lap the whole time. I was lucky that the bus driver and the passengers were very nice. Everybody showed me such respect when they learned of my plight, especially when they saw my daughter in that state. I took her to Tirana so that I could say to myself, yes, you did everything you possibly could for her. I had taken a few quinces, some walnuts, and apples for the doctors, but at the end of the day, they were only people the same as us. If you gift them something, they look at your case differently. This was the third time. Third time lucky?! Perhaps luck will be on our side this time. Luck turned out to be a meaningless word, like hope and sympathy. Yes, they saw us in Tirana and provided their services, but that is about all they had to offer. Once again, they recommended that I find a way of getting her treated abroad. I filled in all the applications. I sent letters to the First Secretary, the Minister of Health, and a host of other officials. This is what I was instructed to do. It's all right for them; life is rosy for them. They couldn't give a toss about my little girl. And who is Rushan to the likes of them at the end of the day? Who am I? A loser, a poor cart driver. Who am I after everything is said and done? You tell me, Avzi…and fill that glass again, will you?" Rushan shouted, waving the empty glass in Avzi's face.

"No, I'm not pouring you another drop.!"

"What, you too, like the other high and mighty up there, slamming the door in my face?! We are cousins, don't forget, and I'm paying you, so it's your job…"

"Have it your way then, but keep that mouth of yours shut, or you'll get us all into trouble," Avzi retorted.

"Do you want to know a secret?" Rushan rambled, "I have been thinking about it when I'm asleep or trundling along in my cart, and all those hours on the bus. I wouldn't care if my daughter grew up to be someone like Minushe, just as long as she were healthy!"

Avzi let out a long sigh. Minushe was a young girl from the neighbouring village. She was an absolute stunner. Full of life, cheeky, very friendly, and somewhat the darling of the village. She knew the power of her looks. That was obvious in the care she devoted to what she wore, her hairstyles, the way she moved, and those tantalizing looks from eyes the colour of the silver-flecked pebbles on the riverbed. She went to the Secondary School for Agriculture in the city and was engaged to be married to an agronomist from the city too. They called him Duro. Martin had seen Duro. He was slightly tubby and had this naïve look about him. Perhaps he was more reserved than he should have been. It was as if people couldn't wait for Minushe's wedding.

Then, one day, the news spread that she had up and left with a soldier from Elbasan. They said she had fallen in love with him and they had been secretly meeting in the city. She had walked out on Duro leaving him twiddling his thumbs. Minushe's name was on everyone's lips for so long. They claimed that she had fallen pregnant with the soldier and that not even a bullet could atone for such disgrace. How many times was it repeated back then that her brother, Fisnik, had sworn to kill her? Martin recalled how everyone said that her family had closed the doors of their house to the world from the shame of it all. The shame had sprung roots and was throttling everyone. Her brother Fisnik had set out for Elbasan two or so months later. They all waited for news of an unprecedented murder. But this did not happen. But Fisnik had found reconciliation with his sister for unknown reasons. However, he did not set foot in his village for years. To the village girls, Minushe was the symbol of the black cat. "Better six feet under than be like Minushe," muttered the old women, the mothers, the girls, everyone. Rushan was the only one who said that night, in a drunken stupor, "I wouldn't care if my daughter became another Minushe as long as she was healthy.!

"Another shot, Avzi!"

"You have had enough!"

"Just one wee shot, and I'll be gone back to spending the night agonizing over my poor, disabled daughter, back to the bane of my life, to my poor little girl. All the other girls of this world dream in their sleep. My little girl, however, lies suffering in her lameness. If you want to know, I think we are all invalids, spread out all around the globe. We are in a stranglehold of lameness; we hardly know whether we are breathing. My old ginger-tufted horse breathes, but he doesn't know lameness; no one does. One more, please."

"You are taking it too far, Rushan! Keep your voice down because even the walls have eyes and ears. The mouths that blabber beyond these walls are treacherous," Avzi whispered urgently in his ear, trying to scare Rushan into calming down.

"Raki is all I want; give it to me; I want to drink like all the lame do. Here's to lameness! May it rot in hell!" Rushan roared at the top of his voice.

The last straggling customers sitting at the table by the window stood up and left. The club was empty, and the darkness of the night crept inside.

"I'm closing up now, Rushan, It's late."

"How about one tiny one for the road, for God's sake! I swear on my son's head, it'll be the last one. One to all the lameness out there! May it live, and may it rot in hell!"

Avzi was aware of the folk expression, 'Even the idiot gives way to the drunkard,' so cajoling and pushing him, he finally got Rushan out of the club. In the village, only the occasional barking of a dog punctured the silence and the darkness and Rushan's drunken shouts of "Long live lameness! Down with lameness!"

Martin would never forget the first time he met Piro…

"Hey, you there, boy. Come a little closer. Come on, move it, there's no time. What's your name? What's your father's name?"

"My name is Martin. I'm Mark Guri's son. I stay with my Uncle Fran Guri for the summer holidays," Martin responded nervously, feeling an emptiness in the pit of his stomach.

"Very good, Martin. Here, take this letter to the Chairman of the Council, Comrade Hazis. Do you know who that is? You are to hand it to him alone. Off you go then; he will be in the office at the Cooperative Center. Do you know where that is?"

"Yes, of course," Martin replied, very quick on the uptake as if trying to flee from this man whose speech cracked like rounds of ammunition rather than words.

That sound originated from the depths of times long gone, from the Twilight Zone of the mountain gorges in the grip of Winter, and from the voids of the Inferno. In the narrow yard of the house belonging to the cart driver Rushan, I got a good look at the man everybody liked, who cracked jokes with my grandmother, usually good-humouredly badmouthing my father. I knew that Rushan's quips were harmless and void of any traces of irony or goading. Deep down, I could tell that my father and Rushan were close, childhood besties, real mates, as they say. Rushan was surrounded by his children, a total of eight little boys and girls; Rushan's wife was trying to appease them with motherly sweet talk and sugar-coated words; Rushan's mother, hunched frozen, in the corner of the yard, was on the verge of collapse, her black head scarf untied and all askew. She looked like a mad woman. She was speechless. Like an ice statue, a congealed autumn leaf hung from a branch, still in the clutches of winter, a branch which the sparrows went about their business of soiling. On the other side of the yard, under the grim shadow of the policemen, was Rushan, her only son. As my Granny used to recount, she had raised him alone in the face of indescribable hardship. Rushan was also frozen, like some giant shapeless, featureless stalagmite. I was waiting to hear him shout and yell that even if he had stolen something, it was from…

These thoughts raced through Martin's mind with growing agitation, and he could hardly breathe. His throat tightened from the anxiety, and he could scarcely feel his limbs.

He remembered the state he was in when he reached Chairman Hazis's office, which was not all that far away. He had knocked and waited.

"Come in," said a voice from inside. Martin remembered pushing gingerly on the door and opening it cautiously. He was face-to-face with Chairman Hazis, a person of considerable clout, but he had heard people speak well of him.

"What is it, boy? The sweat is dripping off you. You'll catch a cold if you're not careful."

Martin looked at him, astonished. *Is he pretending he doesn't know anything?* he asked himself if what was unfolding in Rushan's yard was the accepted norm, not at all out of the ordinary! *How can this person keep his cool when someone a stone's throw away is being arrested in front of his mother, his wife, and his children?!* He took in the other people in the office conversing with the Chairman, the cracked and broken concrete floor, perhaps due to the cold, and shifted his gaze to the bloodshot eyes of Chairman Hazis. No idea why, but Martin had a feeling that Chairman Hazis would save Rushan, at least, insist they held off with the arrest till a little later, at least until they got to the bottom of this whole affair or until his children were a little older, or perhaps after his aged mother departed from this life. Chairman Hazis could and would come to Rushan's assistance to get them to forgive him for the sake of all his children, his poor little disabled daughter.

He pulled himself together. Taking the letter the local Internal Affairs Officer had given him out of his pocket, he placed it in the Chairman's outstretched hand.

"This was given to me to deliver to you. They told me to say that this was an urgent matter," Martin blurted out in a shaky voice.

"Who gave it to you?" he asked, ripping the letter open. When his eyes scanned the writing, he turned to the others in the office, "You're going to have to excuse me, but I must cut this short as something urgent has cropped up. I believe that I won't be too long. Or, better still, let's continue our talk tomorrow; it can wait till then," he said, standing up and shaking hands with those present without really paying attention and obviously in haste. "I am sorry, but this cannot wait. Ahh, well, what can you do? This is what happens when you're Chairman of the Council." He walked out. Martin watched as he walked away. He saw him hurrying his steps until he disappeared around the corner on the track, which led to Rushan's place. Curiosity got the better of him, and Martin ran after him. He wanted to see what would happen. Martin had a clear view of him in the garden of Rushan's house with its heavy old iron gate bordering the track. He stood there exchanging a few words with Piro and could discern the man's swagger from afar. There was no gesturing;

their faces were very close; it was almost like a mouth-to-ear conversation, with words like whiplashes of the wind or globules of silent rain. Martin could tell that the conversation was not going smoothly. It was stuck just like Rushan's cart would get stuck in the mud when he transported the loaves of bread up to the village shop built on a hill slope as if to deliberately make things harder for Rushan. The rain had harrowed deep troughs into the mud track, and his cart would often sink into them. He could only imagine what they were saying by the movement of their lips, the body language, the sly exchange of looks. The Chairman then shrugged his shoulders and looked around, searching for something that the darkness had unexpectedly shrouded. He let out a long, heavy sigh and exited the yard as he had entered. He turned his back and walked away from the Internal Affairs officer of the zone, the police, Rushan, his wife, mother, and children, who were all huddled together in that tiny, pitiful yard.

"Take him!" ordered Piro, the Internal Affairs officer. He walked out of the yard and climbed into the jeep, which had been left running the whole time they were there.

Clinging to their mother, Martin heard the children's cries and pleas. She stood there as if struck by lightning, rooted to the spot as if the life was draining from her face. Martin then saw Rushan's mother approaching the gate, tears streaming down her deeply wrinkled cheeks, lifting the right-hand corner of her scarf to try and check the tears. This old ruin of a house stood apart from the rest of the village. The inhabitants of this house were also somewhat separate from the village folk except Rushan, who was known to and well-liked by everyone.

Rushan was sentenced back then; he was made an example of before everyone. They brought him back to the small square near the Council Chairman's office a few weeks later. He was handcuffed. He was haggard and drained. His shaven head gave him an ashen appearance, and the look of repentance on his pale and unshaven face was clear for everyone to see. They didn't let anyone approach him in the square, not even his mother, children, or wife. To Martin's surprise, his wife stood detached from the crowd, the aged grandmother of those terrified children. Someone shooed all the children in the crowd away. Martin remembered how curiosity got the better of him, and he dodged them, pushing his way in at one side to an even better vantage point than previously. *I have a right to be here anyway, he thought because I was present on the day Rushan was arrested, I was the one who took the letter to Chairman Hazis…*and there was no end to his excuses.

Martin's gaze shifted from the hazy silhouette of Rushan's mother to the figure of his shattered, wiped-out wife, who stood there silent and bent from the weight of it all. Those two petrified figures seemed to form a vast wasteland of ordeals and hardships. Almost everyone gathered there in the square that day experienced a feeling of numbness as if an icy frost had descended on them, although it was summer.

The occasional person said, "Serve them right. He had begun to talk a little too much for everyone's liking; he got what was coming to him. He was a cart driver and had everything he needed."

Others whispered, "It's such a pity, the poor guy. A bunch of children, too. His poor mother is still alive to witness this. There's that disabled daughter; it breaks your heart to see her. How is it possible nobody considered what would become of them? The slightest step out of place and look where you end up…Anyhow, the children have their lives ahead of them, but poor old Rushan, how is it possible that the pencil stopped at his name?!"

A tall, handsome man, well-suited and booted, stern-looking, blush-coloured complexion and layers of hair meticulously combed and swept up on top of his head, began questioning Rushan. His tone was curt, but he articulated his words very clearly. This was the Prosecutor, the first time Martin had ever set eyes on a prosecutor.

"This enemy of the Party and people," the Prosecutor was saying, pointing straight at poor Rushan, "does not like our people's power. With his venomous words, he tried to drive wedges into the spokes of the wheels of our people's power, but vigilance, the revolutionary spirit of the people, and the party are strong!"

The crowd listened without so much as a murmur. To Martin, it seemed that while the Prosecutor was speaking, the air, the wind, the trees, the clover in the fields, the leaves, the birds around them froze. Rushan was the only thing that seemed to be slowly thawing out. He raised his head; his eyes dilated so much that Martin thought they would pop out of his head under the weight of his wounded pride. He thought Rushan would speak, but he looked around, completely dazed. Finally, he murmured, "Please find it in your hearts to forgive me...," and he stared at the ground at the feet of his children, his mother; his imploring gaze was fastened on his wife as if he wanted to say, *"I have left you with so many troubles weighing on your shoulders, I am so sorry, how are you going to make it, you poor thing?"* His eyes brimming with tears, he gazed at his fellow villagers: *"You all know me; how could I possibly bring down the people's power? Me, the cooperative's cart driver, barely literate and with so many grievous problems!"*

Martin couldn't get out of his head Rushan's heartbreaking plea, "Please find it in your hearts to forgive me..."

"Justice, the dictatorship of the proletariat, the party, and Comrade Ramiz..." the Prosecutor had droned on, but Martin had covered his ears with his hands so he couldn't hear any more of that public, people's trial. Running up to the back door of the house, his grandmother's voice had brought him back to earth.

"Good grief, boy, wait. Let me give you some water, and I hope you choke on it!" his grandmother said, thrusting the jug of water into his hands.

Martin's mind was a bedlam of different scenes. Events accumulated and then dispersed as if they moved to the rhythm of the clip-clop of Rushan's horse, through the mud, over the tar seal, up the slopes to the village bakery, down past the yard of his grandmother's house, or past Rushan's house which he hadn't dared look at for the past weeks. Those years were cursed, the late Eighties, looks of alarm and dread, fearful households trembling beneath the weight of those strange, grotesque events.

Martin remembered that day only too well; he remembered that Piro, the Internal Affairs officer, was not with the delegated team that brought Rushan in as if to intimidate the others. Perhaps he had not wanted to come, or possibly his superiors had decided to be there. When the bosses attend, the best Piro could do would be to skunk along the sidelines, that shapeless silhouette of his, but forever sharp-eyed and attentive. *What if he had been sent to arrest another victim like Rushan?* That thought stuck in Martin's mind, and he remembered it very clearly.

For a long time afterward, Martin was to remember how they took Rushan away. That terrifying vehicle, covered in black canvas, disappeared behind the last corner, raising dust clouds of memories and possibly clouds of oblivion. The villagers dispersed, and on the morrow, or perhaps even on that day, they went about their business as usual.

They had sentenced Rushan to eight years imprisonment for propaganda against the State. "A reduced sentence," they had said, "due to an admission of guilt of committing this crime and his display of repentance, and also for the sake of the children and their difficult economic circumstances." At that time, and for the first time, Martin had understood that there were quite a few "80 lek persons" in the village. This is what informants for the State "Sigurimi" (Intelligence Service) were known as, or the collaborators who worked for the cogs in this structure, like Pirro.

More than two years into Rushan's sentence, which he was serving for "propaganda against the State, and working to topple the people's power," his invalid daughter passed away. It was on an autumn day that Martin heard about her demise. Martin was not in the village; summer had long gone, but the news found him in his home in Tirana. "It is probably for the best; she suffered so much, worse than a worm under a stone," the villagers said. Martin remembered poor Rushan and his drunken cries, "Long live infirmity, Down with Infirmity! People claimed that when he learned of the death of his daughter, he had not only said, "I would rather my daughter had been another Minushe," but he had added that if only she were alive, he would not have cared if she was the biggest whore ever. They did not approve his request to attend her funeral. She was no longer in any of Rushan's worlds, not the world on this side of the world beyond.

Drained by the effort to recall this grim story, Martin had floated off into "the lesser beyond" and had fallen asleep.

Chapter III
A bitter cup of coffee

After an almost sleepless night, plagued by dreams, imaginings, remembering, temptation, prejudices, and physical and psychological fatigue, Martin left the house and set out for the office. *"A new day is bearing old wounds,"* he murmured to himself, Arjana's menacing message still uppermost in his thoughts.

For the first time, walking toward his office, he began to weigh the pros and cons of his long-ago decision regarding his vocation. If he had chosen a profile in a different field of science, he would not have faced harrowing unknowns almost daily. Moreover, he would not have been confronted with constant threats, culminating with Arjana's intimidation…

Martin's childhood had been nothing out of the usual, no different than that of anyone else who lived and grew up in the years of the communist regime. His father, Mark, had been an officer in the Armed Forces, and his mother, a nurse at the hospital. There were two children, Martin and his younger sister, Adisa. In those years, with parents employed in these occupations, the family led a normal life where the general belief was that basic requirements were fulfilled. It was very fortunate that his father spent his entire career in the capital city, apart from a short stint when Martin was a teenager, and the family was transferred to "V," a town in the north of the country for around one and a half years.

When the time came for Martin to continue higher studies, Mark insisted that Martin join the Military Academy. Neither Martin nor his mother liked this idea. Martin's excellent results at secondary school and the family's sound biography were in Martin's favour if he wished to continue his studies in Law. Law was a sought-after profession back then, especially for families of "sound political background."

The moment he completed higher studies, Martin was appointed to the position of investigator with the Judicial Police in the capital, thus anchoring himself firmly in a professional career. His passion and acumen for the job were noted straight away as added value to his professional profile, and his superiors soon charged him with the task of heading the structure of the Judicial Police for a period of several years until the President of the Republic decreed him as a State Prosecutor, which became the direction he took in the following years. He had only been transferred once, for a period of two years, to the southern city of "J".

Martin was now a man of mature age, approaching his fifties, and was known as one of the most successful penalizing prosecutors.

A man of average height and build, Martin had dark facial features, black hair with the first hints of grey, a straight nose, vibrant black eyes beneath free-flowing eyebrows, a broad forehead, and a distinct dimpled chin. Martin cut the figure of a good-looking man, which was in line with the appraisal his colleagues made, too. Martin rarely laughed, but when it happened, a set of regular, well-kept teeth instantly materialized in an oval mouth, all adding to his overall attractive appearance.

He always wore a suit and tie, lending him a more formidable look that imposed seriousness in communication with him. He was not an outgoing social type. Rarely would he be seen having coffee with strangers or spontaneous encounters. Sometimes, he would sit down with colleagues of the Law Faculty of the University, where he was involved in lecturing or with police investigators. He preferred to keep to himself and devote his time to many open cases rather than in coffee shops or at lunches and dinners, even though there was no end to daily invitations. His life on the job was choc-a-bloc with occurrences, human predicaments, and tragedies, often appearing on television screens as scoops.

Behind every television scoop, however, lurked a tragedy or drama, at the heart of which there was a need for justice, and this began with the investigation, finding evidence and securing it, contacting witnesses and putting measures in place to guard their lives, weeding out all false information, and ensuring that all criteria are met in the gathering of evidence. All this was invisible to most, but for the professionals, this entailed a vast amount of painstaking work, demanding staying power, wit, capability, care, and professionalism, comparable to the work of a surgeon in the operating theatre to save a patient's life. Perhaps a surgical blunder can be rectified when symptoms of the error are detected in the patient, but a flawed investigation leads to a flawed delivery of justice with fatal consequences not only for the defendant but for many other people in his family and social circles. This was never far from Martin's mind as he did his best to be as fair and honest as possible in his work and assess people on merit, nothing more, nothing less. He now knew only too well, and experience had taught him that justice called for unrelenting work. He spent most of the day working in his office, apart from when he had scheduled meetings. You were sure to find him leafing through files and folders, underlining things, wholly absorbed, reading what was there and what was between the lines in the many piles of material spread out over his entire desktop, searching for legal arguments in the ledgers on jurisprudence or going yet again through forensic reports and evidence. On the dates set for trial sittings, he meticulously prepared everything he would need from the respective files. He went before the judges, feeling somewhat like he did in his student years during university examinations because every sitting constituted a professional and humane challenge to him. He always aimed to be punctual regarding the timetables for the sittings and every other planned event. As soon as he completed his work in the courtroom, he would return to his office, where he could closely follow all penal processes he was working on. Certain cases were real hot potatoes because of the specific range of issues they covered and, sometimes, due to the risk of the public impact they carried. Legal deadlines were on you before you knew it, compelling him to make good use of every minute that came and went. Timely planning was his professional secret, meaning his job had no set working hours. He worked extremely hard at the office and in his studio at home to ensure he never missed a single legal deadline.

"It's the same as with a surgeon who cannot be late for a patient's operation; neither should the prosecutor or the judge miss legal and procedural deadlines for the defendant and the victims in a process," Martin would say to his colleagues and students.

You're not a politician for explaining and inspiring. You are a prosecutor. You follow up on facts and evidence, not on outbursts and passions—an inner voice constantly repeated in his head. However, he was not immune to compassion. He was a human being with his sentiments and dreams. He had a family, friends, and colleagues from whom he drew motivation to remain a decent human being.

On one such day, faced with an overload of work and emotions and feeling the need for a coffee with friends, Martin noticed Sokol Prroni walking toward him, a friend and colleague of many years. He felt an almost infantile urge well up inside him to "open up" to a friend, nearly the same age as his father, not to confess anything or peddle a sob story, but to share a little time with him, like those minutes you "steal" from exams or when you dodge a dental appointment. They nodded to each other from a distance, and instinctively Martin gestured toward the coffee shop next to the Offices of the Prosecution. With a chuckle, Sokol nodded in agreement and turned in that direction. They exchanged the usual greetings, but Sokol quickly picked up on the fact that something was bothering Martin; he was not his usual self, the Martin that Sokol knew so well.

"Looks like you've been burning the midnight oil again and forgotten to get some sleep," he said jokingly.

"To tell the truth, you are not far wrong," Martin replied, adding, "That's why I thought we could have a coffee to start the day right."

"It's quite a while since we caught up over coffee, but you've been up to your neck with work, and I've been busy, too. I'm working with the Ministry on those new Codes they're asking for. I get home very late and I'm out the door first thing in the morning. Comes with the territory… what can I say…"

After their coffees came, Sokol asked, "Do you have a sitting today?"

"No, not today, but tomorrow, Friday, I have a sitting for the case of that Boja guy…" Martin replied quietly.

"I've heard about it. But we have every confidence in you; you're very good at wrapping things up cleanly and leaving no loose ends," Sokol continued.

"Eh, you never know what might crop up and then…" Martin responded irritably.

"Is there a problem? Is something wrong?" Sokol asked attentively.

"No, not at all; I just meant, in general," Martin replied casually, gazing out beyond the glass shop front as if trying to shake off the shadow of Arjana.

"I remember telling you before, when you're working such cases as this, leave your emotions out of it. When you walk into the Prosecutor's Office, you have left all emotions behind in the hallway of your home," Sokol said.

Sokol had been a prosecutor for a very long time. His experience spanning the period from the past regime and the years of a democratic system had made him a person with a comprehensive world outlook and a great deal of knowledge, but above all this, experience had made him fair, a man who had used justice solely as a means of delivering justice. Irrespective of the ideological dogma, he remained glued to books on local and foreign Law, aiming to reach perfection within what appeared to be the absurdity of so-called "people's justice."

"Look here, Martin, I can see you seem disheartened today, and I can sense that you are assessing yourself, wondering if you made the right or the wrong move on taking this course so that I will relate an event from my beginnings as a prosecutor. I discovered that from books to reality, there is a yawning gap, my friend. I had never dreamt that I would come up against what I did in my professional life while discharging my duties back in the years when I poured over those books, preparing for exams. The courtroom is where we score the real marks, in the public's opinion and our awareness of a job well done. And that's why you must keep it firmly in mind that you are nowhere near your countdown time, your withdrawal. I am nearing the end of my career, but you, too, have reached almost halfway, and there is no going back. A good swimmer stays the course."

And he launched into his story, composed and with so much literary colour, the way only he knew how to. Sokol read so much literature that he knew thousands of lines of the works of the most well-known poets by heart. Literature frequently assisted him during court trials in formulating and articulating a world apart from others and the judicial prototypes learned at school. It was a pure pleasure to listen to Sokol.

"...I was new to the job; it was during the first months after graduation, and one day, I received official notice that the request by H.P. for clemency from the death penalty had been rejected. I remember it was a Spring afternoon when they informed me of this. I was the prosecutor defending the charges brought against the accused. Therefore, it was down to me to execute the ruling made. The defendant, who had been given the death penalty, had murdered two young cousins. The murders had been committed for weak motives. The conflict ended in tragedy and had begun in connection with the defendant's sister. I was a very young prosecutor, and at all the court trials, I had passionately aimed to secure the heaviest sentence possible for the person accused of a double homicide. He was a murderer and had to be treated and sentenced as one. The Law stipulates that, as the prosecutor on the case, I had to head the execution group. This was the very first time I found myself in such a situation. I began to feel tremendous sadness, and it was as if this toxic sentiment had poisoned me and circulated throughout my whole being like diseased blood. I retired, went home earlier than usual, and did not exchange a word with anyone that evening. It was prohibited, but even if I had wanted to, I couldn't have shared this anxiety with anyone. I remember lying in bed, but I had no hope of getting any sleep. I couldn't get the face of the accused out of my head. On the other hand, he would meditate on his daily routine in his cell. I would be the one who, minutes before his execution, would have to communicate to him the decision taken that his clemency plea had been refused. What if he had already found out about this decision?! I could imagine him in his cell, handcuffed, sobbing, and trembling, waiting for them to collect him at any moment. Death is a mystery, such a bitter moment, experienced only once. For everyone, without exception, this is the final and the most terrible moment. It was his greatest misfortune to learn from me that he would no longer be in the land of the living a few minutes from now. This demise would not come naturally and mysteriously as it does for everyone else but forewarned and scheduled. We were the ones, the execution team, who were to cut short the life of this man in the name of the Law. And even though we were going to oversee his execution before a firing squad, we would simply report it as the routine carrying out of a court ruling. Dark, depressing feelings had taken hold of my mind and soul. This individual facing execution had taken two lives and deserved to be punished. The old timers always said that God gives life and only He has the right to take it. At one moment, I felt like an executioner, and the next, like someone administering justice. The anxiety was suffocating. The ring of the phone jerked me out of this reverie.

It was midnight on the dot. Strangely, it was a clear and refreshingly cool evening. The voice on the house landline phone said crisply, "Comrade Prosecutor, we are on our way to pick you up. Please be downstairs."

Hurriedly, I threw some clothes on and went down. In the yard in front of the apartment block, I saw the vehicle from the Internal Affairs Branch already parked waiting for me. I was surprised to see the Chief of Police; I couldn't say whether he was composed, but I noticed how hard he was drawing on a cigarette. He was standing on the footpath looking over toward the entrance to the block where I lived. The prisoner, with the police escort, had gone on ahead to the site of the execution. Without a doubt, being removed from his cell in the dead of the night, under tight security precautions, would have been a clear indication to the prisoner of what lay ahead. The top brass of the Police Force had decided the place of execution, not all that far from the city. This was the first time for me. I looked at the Chief of Police, who didn't seem particularly troubled, which made me feel sick. I knew I wasn't well, although I tried hard not to show it. As we drove along, all sorts of thoughts came and went.

In my imagination, that pale face of the prisoner hovered before me. It seemed to be begging me, pleading for our forgiveness. "I am locked away in prison; I'll be there for the rest of my days. I'm like a living corpse anyway, so why can't you let me die when God deems it to be the moment?" I was in complete turmoil!

A few minutes into the drive, the Chief of Police opened a conversation without any connection to the act we were about to perform, at the most in an hour. I wasn't listening at all to what he was saying. I was shocked at the frightening calm he showed. A person was about to die, to be executed, to cease living in my presence before my very eyes. We were about to kill that person. To a certain degree, we were about to commit the act for which he was being executed. He did it instinctively as the result of his internal revolt. We were about to do it based on articles and the right to do so provided for in the law.

He would not be able to see the dawning of the next day. He was only twenty-seven. My heart throbbed painfully. We were going to take the life of an individual who was neither ill nor had he complained about his health. We would do this calmly and coldly, keeping to a rigid protocol. It was just me, with a bunch of individuals in police uniform and a doctor. They seemed to be accustomed to performing this ritual of taking a life. This filled me with sadness. I would have gladly given everything not to be present at this tragedy. It was the penal procedure that made my presence obligatory. Moreover, I had to direct this horrific ritual, something I had only read about in novels. With all these dreadful thoughts swirling around in my head, we reached the appointed place. It was a tiny clearing, fringed by bunches of low-lying bushes, already sporting spring's new, green leaves. The prisoner, handcuffed and encircled by the police escort of six officers, stood there in this tiny clearing. In such cases, the prosecutor delivers the final communication to the prisoner that his plea for clemency has been refused. This is what the law stipulates, and the law was going to be applied to the letter. This was an irreversible protocol—the prisoner. H.P. waited calmly, quite the opposite of what I expected. To me, he seemed to be facing his death like a man, with bravery. Did he realize what was going to happen in a matter of minutes?

I stepped up close and looked deep into those eyes that shone and showed no sign of fear, remorse, or the intention to beg for mercy. I stepped back, embarrassed. I was more terrified of all of this than he was. I spoke to him softly, compassionately, so much so that I barely got the words out:

"Your plea to save your life has been refused." This didn't sound like my voice. I fell silent for a moment because there was no reaction on his part, so I continued. "Therefore, we are here to communicate this to you and to execute the ruling of the Court. My duty requires that I ask what your last words are?"

He was looking straight at me without wavering in the slightest. To his infinite surprise, this person had appeared in front of him in these closing moments of his life and was expressing regret. A person who, every time he had stood opposite him in Court, had been severe and had spoken to him in firm tones, confident and unyielding. The prisoner gave me a look that I will never forget. I saw no tears in those deep, dark eyes. I could feel the tears welling up, and I pulled myself together. The Chief of Police and the execution squad were waiting for me to play out my formal, futile, and fake role to the end. This was required by law. Anway… After gazing in my direction for some time with open contempt, he said, "Prosecutor, I have brought this on myself, this death penalty. I murdered two young men, 20 years of age, which means I do not deserve to live either. My final words are to ask the forgiveness of the parents of the victims whom I have left bereft of their sons." He uttered these words, looked around, and then, staring straight at me, he added, "So, let my father also lose his son." I placed a hand on his shoulder, a gesture that revealed the pain I felt. "Prosecutor, could you please have my cuffs removed so I can enter that world, free and uncuffed?" he said, without taking his eyes off me, which still shone in the dark illuminated by the full moon and a torch one of the police officers was shining on us. I wasn't sure what the rules said about this; this was my first time and a nerve-wracking experience. I didn't waste any more time, but I turned to the Chief of Police and the firing squad, "Remove his handcuffs," I commanded. "Remove them immediately!" From behind me, I noticed the Chief of Police signing that I should not be demanding such a thing.

"Uncuff him!" I ordered again abruptly. In this situation, the young man found the strength to express his gratitude in the look he sent my way. He didn't speak a word, but his eyes said it all. They uncuffed his hands, and they didn't blindfold him. The command was given.

"Fire!"

A dozen shots rang out, many bullets hit home, and he fell to the ground. Instinctively, I moved in his direction as if to try and stop him from falling. He lay there, stretched out on the ground. There was still life in him, and his gaze locked onto me. There was calm and warmth in those eyes. And that is how he passed, this person, until they finally closed his eyes, and the doctor murmured the verdict, "It's over, he gone."

I lifted my gaze to the skies and spoke to God in silence. I prayed and pleaded that He showed mercy to that young man and us. I would have liked God to have sent down bolts of lightning and inclement rain then and there as if to lament the moment in which we had just taken the life of a man. This was a night with clear skies brimming with stars and a full moon, which enabled the illumination of the moment when a man was executed and whose heart had only just ceased to beat. This was when the Penal Code foresaw the death penalty…"

"Martin, I told you this because we have sworn an oath to serve the country and the Law impartially, leaving our conscience to be judged by He who judges us all one day. We are not the ones who make the laws; the only thing we do is implement them, so this being the case, all that is left for us to accomplish is implement them correctly, based on evidence, with conviction and absolute impartiality," Sokol concluded.

"I just had to meet up with you Koli (short for Sokol). I must find the strength not to tremble in my boots when I hear the words, threats, blackmail, exaggerated praise, and intervention by family members," Martin said deep in thought, looking his friend in the eye. After sitting there for quite a while discussing a host of amendments scheduled to be made to the new Penal Code, the two friends parted, promising it would not take them so long to meet up again. Martin walked back to his office, more at ease than when he had left home, although the anxiety Arjana had caused was still with him…

CHAPTER IV
The Surgical Theatre and Justice

Since no one could enter his office before or after him, Martin recoiled at the heavy odour of cigarettes and alcohol as soon as he opened the door. Immediately, he threw the windows open and then flicked on his computer.

He felt more at ease after his coffee with Sokol. Martin's mind wandered: *He experienced his first execution of a prisoner, something similar to medical students standing in front of the corpse of a person at an anatomy lesson or when they operate for the first time. Pain belongs to the patient, but the anxiety, stress, and psychological burden is on the surgeon. In prosecution, the defendant also takes the sentence, and he bears the sentence. Still, the stress, the psychological drain, and the burden of the conscience are borne and endured by the prosecutor or judge. Medicine and justice are two poles at which people surrender and await justice and equal treatment. The patient listens to every syllable the doctor pronounces, as does the defendant before the prosecutor and judge. In medicine, there is an oath framework designed to administer impartial and equal treatment for all patients, irrespective of who they are, and this is called 'The Hippocratic Oath.' In justice, however, what regulates things? Is the legal basis sufficient, or is there a need for a similar oath here, too? In justice, the 'Hypocrite's Oath' often suffices.*

He slumped into the armchair opposite his work desk, his eyes resting on the very fat file on Marjan Boja. To the top right of the dossier, encased in a beautiful frame, looking more alive than ever, was the photo of the deceased Artur Rrasa smiling warmly at him.

Turi (short for Artur) was present; he kept coming back to Martin like a meteor combusting and flaming in the sky, burning out, falling to Earth, only to rise again high into the Universe, falling again, and rising again. A star that will never die out. He would have loved Turi to have married, had children, a family, and lived his life to the fullest. It hurt him deep inside when he thought about how Turi had gone without experiencing the joys of life. From his position on Martin's desktop, Artur seemed to speak to Martin about their school years, shared friends, their families, pretty girls, the weddings of their mutual friends, and stories that made you keel over with laughter.

During his initial years on the job, when Martin worked at the Judicial Police, investigation work was draining and rife with tension due to the intense dynamics of the events and proceedings they covered. Back then, the drive was relentless; he worked day in and day out. This strong friendship with Artur Rasa had its roots in those times. Artur was a more experienced investigator, while Martin was a passionate and uncompromising novice. Artur was forever on the move, energetic, expressive, astute, and productive at his job. Artur's keen intuition and avid commitment solved many challenging cases, even in the knottiest of events. Turi very rapidly became the role model Martin wished to follow. All the nights in the office when they would re-enact all possible crime scenarios remained fresh in his memory. Like a seasoned stage producer, Artur would reconstruct the event strictly as it had been reported. Then, lighting a cigarette, he would sink into a nearby armchair and say through the curling smoke, "Right, I'm the felon, and you're the victim." He would often grab a plastic pistol we used as an office prop and start playing out an investigation's drama. Martin Guri thought that perhaps Turi was not all there when he put on this kind of act for the first time. He reproduced the most unexpected scenes, using his imagination and acting skills, even roaring his head off like Bertold Becht's Arturo Ui. Turi had a way of penetrating the aggressive psychology of criminals. When his imagination reached its climax, he would slump back into the armchair, saying: "Eureka! The motive must have been…"

Martin was convinced that no two other investigators had quite the same dynamics they had and created together so professionally. "When we work a case, we take from the criminal's world. We must know about their world to be effective in our investigations and to be able to deliver a sturdy indictment…." Artur Rasa's words reverberated in Martin's mind. Turi was a brilliant police investigator. Unlike Martin, who made no effort to hide his ambition, he was not motivated by efforts to climb the career ladder in his field. Whenever this subject crept into their conversations, Martin had tried hard to awaken feelings of ambition in his career. Chuckling, Turi would repeat the Albanian saying carved into a wine barrel in the Castle of Petrela, "Whoever lives for a career dies; whoever doesn't also die. I am for enjoying life and drinking the forgotten wine - a career!" How could this have happened? Had he predicted that he would die so soon?

**

It was a summer evening. A gentle breeze wafted in, bringing a welcoming respite to people from the grueling heat of the day. Martin was relaxing on the couch in his sitting room in front of the open balcony doors, gazing out at Mount Dajti in the distance, a giant, sprawling steely-green beetle. He had chosen to stay at home that Saturday. He wanted a break from it all and some time with the boys. They were in their early adolescence, and he was middle-aged. They loved the friendly sparring between one another. Eliza cherished these moments and always pretended to be on Martin's side. The boys were beside themselves with excitement and happiness, hurtling themselves on their parents, hugging and kissing them profusely.

"We're happy when we can "arrest" Dad and keep him at home," Eliza often said.

These were the most poignant family moments when Martin spent a day at home when there was no shop talk. Not even the boys were in a mood to talk about school. They spoke of the films on Netflix, the hacking of digital technology, their favourite songs, and the trends of the time. They often made Martin listen to their preferred songs. The boys quite frequently argued with each other as to which was the trendiest song or the coolest film. They rambled on about books they had read, chiefly in English, with some stories that Martin honestly just did not get at all.

As was regularly the case with him, however, the bitter memories of that blackest of days so many years ago would return, perhaps because he had pangs of guilt over the happiness in his own life…

He was at home on his own when his phone rang. Lazily, he reached out and picked up the phone from where he had dropped it on the bedside table. It was the Operations Room calling, so he answered immediately.

"Mr. Guri, this is the Operations Room calling," the officer's voice had a different ring from other checking-in calls.

"They have just killed Artur Rrasa."

"What did you say?!" Martin yelled.

"I'm sorry, it's true; they have just killed Turi," the officer repeated, his voice failing.

Martin froze; he felt the hair on his skin rise in goosebumps all over his body. From the timbre of the officer's voice, he could feel that he was on the brink of breaking down.

"Artur Rrasa?" Martin mumbled, with the hope that what he had just heard could not be accurate.

"It's him…we were just notified from the scene…where it happened. He was killed…next to his home…he has died. The officer hung up. He had barely managed to deliver this devastating news.

Still holding on to his phone, Martin collapsed on the couch. His legs had packed up beneath him. He sobbed uncontrollably. He prayed that this was all a nightmare and that this benumbing announcement was fake. Dear God! Never in his life had he experienced a blow like this. He got up, tears welling up, splashed some water over his face, got changed, and left for the scene where the killing had happened. How many times had he retraced his steps down this road to meet his best friend? He would be sitting at the little coffee shop on the ground floor of his apartment bloc. This was never to happen again. Martin would never again find him here, would never see him or hear his voice again. Turi was dead. Martin's eyes overflowed with uncontrollable tears of pain. In a matter of minutes, he reached the crime scene. He had driven like a madman. What he saw there at the scene was horrific, appalling. He felt the shivers up and down his spine; his whole being ached from the pain. Turi, this giant of a man, lying motionless on the footpath, his blood still oozing out in tiny rivulets, puddling beneath his body. The bullets had entered his back and had been fatal. His right hand had frozen over his belt where he had holstered his gun. The perfidious volley from behind had cut him down, and he had had no chance to react. The shrieking anguish of it all was visible, tangible, lying there before Martin's eyes. Martin stood there, stunned, at this crossroads of tragedy, in shock, before Artur's lifeless form, incapable of processing any thought about anything. He couldn't bring himself to lift the sheet they had covered him with to see that bloodied face. He didn't want to see him in this state or to carry that image away with him. Martin needed to preserve the likeness of that striking and vibrant face. The tears welled up, overpowering him. His body sagged on trembling knees;

his head rocked between the palms of his hands. Martin felt his back bow agonizingly beneath the burden of grief for the loss of a revered friend and colleague. He refused to believe it, even though the blood-spattered body lay right in front of him. At that moment, he understood in his very bones how high-risk his job was. *Turi was right when he said that with or without a career, people die; with or without power, people die; wealthy or poor, they still die. So why is there so much warring in life? Why?* He gave it a lot of thought. He didn't have the answer. Rhetorical questions kept popping into his head to keep the memory of his friend alive when, in fact, he was no more. Martin looked away, struggling to hold back the tears. Gradually, his sight was focusing. He gazed around him and noticed the crowd gathering beyond the security tape. Although driven by curiosity, even they looked taken aback and shaken. You could read the grief and horror on their faces. The evil hand of crime had been raised against a state prosecutor with alarming daring, endangering public safety, the safety of Artur's neighbours, and other anonymous citizens.

The television cameras arrived on the scene and, from a distance, were trying to take shots of the crime scene. Numerous reporters broadcast live for their media outlets, dishing up various options regarding the event and its circumstances. Most of them focused on the victim, Artur Rrasa, "a martyr of justice," they said, who, sadly, for the first time, was not there to update them on the latest tragic event. He was the "event" this time, and nothing could be more tragic.

Martin looked over at the two officers of the Judicial Police who had begun to carry out crime scene procedures. The Prosecution Office for Serious Crimes had arrived on the scene and were locked in conversation with the forensics experts who took down notes on everything.

Martin felt afresh the twist of the massive knot deep inside his chest, almost suffocating him. He felt an icy chill run through his body. In that second, he wished it were him lying there instead of Artur. Artur's death was almost too much for him to bear. He could only picture his friend, who was forever full of life and dynamic. His mind refused to accept that he had gone. And then, everything seemed to be shoved out of his mind only to be replaced by a huge question mark: who had snatched the life of Artur Rrasa?

They lifted the body from the scene, and it was sent to the morgue. Night had fallen and reigned supreme. Martin felt his very soul was in its grip. The soul should be free to fly and savour the night's velvety beauty, not its dark depths. The stark neon streetlights pierced into the surroundings of the crime scene, where work continued to examine and identify everything. Martin joined the group of investigators to ensure that all was accurately documented. 17 Kalashnikov cartridges were collected as forensic evidence. Volleys of bullets had racked the body of the deceased. These bullets were the only things that could have terminated Artur's love of life; it was these bullets that brought up short all that energy. A pool of congealed blood still marked the spot on the footpath, but after all the forensic samples were taken, it too would evaporate and disappear, leaving nothing behind. Several citizens who had witnessed the crime were contacted, but they were too terrified to speak. They maintained that they hadn't seen a thing but that they had heard the shots. Obviously, they did not want to be involved in occurrences like this. They were frightened. Police officers had also begun to panic due to a spate of serious offenses that had occurred over the past months. A good number of them had resigned from the Force. The situation was dire. In such a chaotic situation, public safety, stability, and order seemed like an urban legend, and public security was like some distant dream.

Roughly seventy meters from the crime scene, at the entrance to a dark alleyway, Martin, who had also joined the search to comb the site, caught sight of a mask and a pair of gloves discarded beside a rubbish can. He informed the lead investigator and forensics. He was careful not to touch anything. Wearing the correct kit, the experts carefully lifted the gloves, scrutinizing them closely. They found strands of hair inside the woollen hat, which they bagged with special care and described and recorded in the evidence documentation. Scraps of evidence were sealed into small plastic bags and containers to be examined at the Forensics Laboratory.

Sometime later, when the examination of the crime scene was completed, Martin left in his car for the morgue, where Turi's relatives had arrived. It was an indescribably horrific night that he would never forget. It was late. He wondered why the streets seemed so deserted. How many times had he gone to the morgue together with Turi and the forensic experts to examine victims of murders they were investigating? And now, it was his body Martin was to examine. Martin didn't go into the morgue. He felt he was unable to look down upon that lifeless face. Martin wanted to hang on to the memory of his friend forever, full of life and strength. Now, Artur was a hero. A deceased hero. Living heroes are needed more than ever today. Deceased heroes were of no use to anyone, Martin thought, even less so Martin.

Memories of poignant and painful moments flooded Martin's memory. It seemed that any will to work had gone together with Artur. In a certain sense, Artur was his mentor on this career path Martin had chosen, and only sleeping hours had divided them. Who knows how many events and files they had drafted together? Who knows how many cups of coffee they had consumed over tension-filled discussions about work?

The reenactments of crimes the two of them had staged in the office, where Turi always took on the role of the offender, flashed before his mind's eye. How would he do the acting now? He needed Artur alive, "the criminalistic actor" for whom there was no criminal situation he could not unravel.

He could hear his inner voice reply, *No, Martin Guri, that is certainly not the way to think; that's surrendering to evil. Who would be left to battle crime if everyone was to feel like that? Who would be the police officer, the detective, the prosecutor, the correctional officer? All of them are unpleasant jobs at the best, but jobs that must be done nonetheless; otherwise, society will expire.*

He breathed in deeply. His mind wandered again to the pathologists in the morgues who performed all kinds of autopsies on bodies riddled by bullets or slit open with knives, funeral undertakers who see nothing but death and pain and tears all day, every day, he thought of the grave diggers, forever opening or filling graves and sighing like lost souls:

See? There are even worse jobs, but someone must do them! Who would bury us otherwise?

The way his mind wandered frightened him. He didn't think he could take any more. Lighting a cigarette, he imagined Turi in front of him. "Right, I'm the criminal, you're the victim." That voice echoed in his ears. This was no enactment of a crime, no dream; this was reality.

On the morrow of this tragic occurrence, the turnout at the funeral was overwhelming. The highest-ranking officers of the state Police paid their respects and gave speeches. Artur was posthumously awarded the distinction "Matyre of the Homeland." The funeral procession was outstanding. *We're so good at organizing ceremonies for police officers who have fallen on duty. He accomplished brilliant work when he was alive, and no one uttered a good word. How sad is that? A great deal of attention is devoted to a police officer at two specific moments: when a plan is being drawn up to get rid of him and when his funeral is organized. The actors differ, but in both instances, they are deadly serious.*

Buckling under the burden of these bitter thoughts, Martin felt utterly drained; he ached to be alone, not another soul around him, so that he could converse with Artur, now of that other world beyond Eternity.

…He couldn't stop the inevitable any longer, so he answered Eliza's call. She had known Artur, but Martin had spoken of him so much that Eliza felt she knew everything about him. She had profoundly understood that there was a deep-going connection between Martin and Artur. And now, Artur no longer lived.

"What am I to do, Eliza?" he had asked his wife as if caught in a trap.

"You're going to have to find double the strength for yourself and Turi," she said, trying to console him. Exhausted by the shock of it all, the sheer weight of his feelings, his head pounding as if someone had hit him with something hard, Eliza tenderly lowered his head to her bosom, as only she knew how to do. It was here that Martin found refuge, where he always found peace, repose, and comfort.

Although during a tough patch, the experience gained from working with Artur made Martin an even better investigator. Entirely different characters, Turi's dynamic nature had drawn a more thoughtful Martin into its vortex, making him even more determined and unwavering in protecting the truth, which no one ever wanted.

For a long time, he struggled to come to terms with losing his mate and work associate. To him, this was a true-life loss, as if a part of his very being was lost.

In all his later activity, as a prosecutor too, Martin had been severe in sentencing offenders charged with murder. They all seemed identical to him, all these killers. And every time, he would recall Turi and his execution. In every murder case he took on, Artur was always in his thoughts. He heard his voice like a throbbing call for revenge. He could see him, full of laughter, alive with enthusiasm, desperate, at times, furious and taunt with tension, just as he had known him. Martin constantly heard that teeth-grinding noise when, in fits of frustration, Turi's jaws would clamp shut. This was not infrequent for Artur, who had such passion and a strong sense of fairness.

Every time Martin attended the Police Academy to lecture on Crime and Penal Law for new students, Artur Rrasa's bust in bronze was there. He looked magnificent, that bitter smile playing on his lips. He was a source of inspiration for every student at the Police Academy. To Martin, as a close friend of his, Turi was nothing but someone who had passed away and whom he missed tremendously: a champion of upholding the Law, cut down by the bullets of crime. Now, he was merely a number, someone who had been betrayed and left alone to fend for himself by the State and wily Justice, to which he had also belonged.

To Martin, there was something infinitely sad about the sculptured bust. It was a voiceless silhouette staring into the shadows that flittered in and out of there. It was a bust without a voice, unrelenting in its determination never to reveal its true story to the students. That would demoralize them before even embarking on their careers. Although very rarely, it had happened that, late at night, Martin Guri had wandered over, stood beside that cold sculpture, and lit a cigarette. It was as if he tried to lend warmth to it from the tobacco's red-hot ring as he hungrily drew on it to create that suffocating smoke cloud. He wanted to shout at the top of his lungs that *the cigarette was invented so that people didn't go insane.* Then, again, in the thick tobacco smoke, he improvised his role as if speaking to the statue. He was cautious not to be seen at night, so no one thought he had gone mad, but he found renewed strength there to push forward. He always recalled how he had once told his friend the saying of an American police officer, "When standing in front of the mirror in the morning shaving, every day the policeman acknowledges himself as if he is seeing his reflection for the last time." During those moments beside the bust, Artur seemed to say to him, "You have the great fortune to be alive; don't waste your life. Do what you do best with dedication. Do what I would have done, too."

***

By bringing stimulating episodes and moments of his professional journey to his attention, Martin had become absorbed again and found a degree of peace. The conversation he had had with Sokol that morning nourished this. Unexpectedly, his line of thought was interrupted by Andi, his only sister's son, who walked into his office. Andi was in his thirties, a cherry person. He had made it a habit to drop in to say hello. He was an architect. They embraced and exchanged greetings. Martin always made an effort to match Andi's sunny nature. When all the updating and small talk customary for these meetings had run out, Andi handed Martin a letter in an envelope.

"It's for you," he said, placing it in his hand.

When he entered the office, Martin never thought for one moment that Andi's presence there had to do with business. Andi always showed him affection and special awareness.

Somewhat surprised, Martin took the envelope and opened it immediately. He read that short letter eagerly. That brief text threw him, his whole being, completely. Suddenly, he was very anxious and felt the colour drain from his face. The office ceiling reeled overhead. He read the letter in silence with Andi standing before him. Instinctively, he asked:

"Who gave you this envelope?"

"The bosses of the company I work for," Andi replied, feeling awkward and confused by Martin's instant reaction. The young man stood there, confused but also curious to learn what the letter said.

"I've never asked who the company owners you work for are, Andi?" Martin asked, struggling to gather his wits.

"They are based outside of the country, so I don't know them," Andi said, adding, "They rarely come to Tirana. They are seriously affluent and powerful in the business. They summoned me to the central offices today and asked about you. I told them you are my Uncle. They already knew that because they asked if I would deliver this letter to you, so here I am."

Baffled, his sentences came out erratically, and he was nervous that he had done something he should not have. He fell silent momentarily but then added, "Have I made a mistake, Uncle Martin? I am so sorry; I didn't give it a second thought. I never dreamt it would cause concern. I thought it might have to do with looking at a new apartment. What is it about? "

"There's no problem," Martin replied drily, "we'll talk another time."

They said goodbye, and Andi left the office bewildered, not knowing what else to say. Martin collapsed into the armchair, staggered by how things were entangled. He sat there for some time analyzing the text of this letter in depth. He felt his gaze grow misty. The letter said: *"Marjan Boja is a friend of ours. We must assist him get out of prison. It is within your remit to do this. You will be compensated. Within the "Horizon" complex, under construction in the center of Tirana, 500 square meters of building carry your name. Via the bearer of this letter, who is ignorant of its content, you can send your trusted person with whom we can sign a Deed of Gift. This property's value is 1.5 million euros. If you do not prefer property, the value is ready in cash. Your two sons need to be brought up well, not like Marjan. Tomorrow is the test and an opportunity that will never come your way again."*

He shuddered again. Never in his life had he been sent such a letter. How dare they?! It all flashed back through his mind: the toil, sleeplessness, sacrifice, Turi's blood, the temptations, pressures, despair, the failures, the successes… *"I am not interested, and I don't need anything. The indictment is ready,"* he said to himself defiantly. Everything seemed to be whirling around in his head like the propellor of an aircraft lifting him upwards.

Like a bolt out of the blue, they had dared and found the conduit to bear their offer. A very generous and tempting offer laced with poison. They could choose another method, pay somebody a small amount to have him permanently removed from this world. In this environment, saturated with despair, bullets cost far less than the millions they were offering to get a criminal released from prison. The metastasizes of organized crime have sprouted roots everywhere, penetrating everything and implicating anyone they require, Martin thought in despair.

What was the connection between these affluent and influential people and Marjan Boja?

Unconsciously, most likely, but with breath-taking stupidity his nephew Andi had put himself at the service of his bosses. He had no idea how convoluted and thorny these things are. It was unknown who his employers were, where they were from, and how they had made all this wealth. Based on day-to-day business, files, and the information Martin had, he learned every day that the ties these new, young capitalists had were frightening. Their presence cast a very long shadow. They corrupted and/or seized everything they needed. Their connections with Members of Parliament, government officials, Mayors, Police Chiefs, and media outlet owners created ample space for them to build and set up businesses wherever they wished, and the heart of Tirana was no exception. The formula they had functioned like a marvel: something that cannot be done with money, can be done with immense amounts of money.

Arjana was not the only one chipping away at Martin's peace of mind. His state of mind was in a turmoil. Compared with this letter, Arjana's interest and efforts now seemed more humane and natural. He tried to imagine the faces of these invisible bosses who hatched plans and executed their ideas without so much as batting an eyelid. He could see them seated in their lavish offices, serviced by carefully selected personnel, the massive work tables covered in business projects. He saw them seated in the most expensive restaurants, discussing their outrageous objectives, both presumptuous and criminal. They made decisions to implement these projects beneath the spiralling smoke of expensive cigars, under the soothing effect of first-class whisky and cocaine. It is in these luxurious offices that they consult with state officials and MPs regarding their business concepts. It is here that properties and monies are divvied up. It is here that the finishing touches are put to the capital's urban development. And why not? It is here those final decisions are made on appointing people to top state positions and where plans are devised to have people who obstruct the realization of these plans executed.

If there was money in the offering, it meant nothing to them to switch to Plan B. Pay someone to eliminate a prosecutor! That was a very inexpensive offer. It cost them nothing to create an incident and an Albanian Falcone! *"Why don't they do something useful instead of embarking on a course like this driven by their insanities?"* Martin Guri muttered.

The cigarette smoke had created an oppressive environment in Martin's office, and the layers of smoke were suffocating him. *"Your two sons need to be brought up well, not like Marjani,"* Martin mumbled to himself. *They have done their homework and found out I have two sons. They mention this in the letter…"* He felt the knife turn deep down in his heart. The letter was not simply an inducement to accept a bribe. It went far more profound than that. They were angling for Martin Guri, waiting for him to take the bait. Martin felt like an offender on death row awaiting execution. Exactly the same as the story Sokol had told him. He could feel the noose was tightening. He could hardly breathe. Take the money or expect the bullets! This is how he interpreted the letter he waved around in the air. He had no idea what his next move would be. He felt entirely alone, face to face with this powerful empire of crime, which had it all: money, fame, power, and strength. To top it off, they were invisible and anonymous, just like the letter's authors. However, their infamy resonated throughout Tirana's coffee shops and bars. People spoke of them like legends. They were characters with prominence and code-names that weaved in and out of the conversations of ordinary citizens like frightening phantoms. They emerged from clandestine criminal activities in Europe and as far away as America. Now, they materialized within their deluxe offices in Tirana bearing business plans, with appointments in place for meetings with the finest architects of Europe, to "develop" this country and increase their revenues, might, and fame. The letter bore no address, no name, and no signature. Electronically written, it bore no other trace of anything. There was no writing on the envelope. However, that had no significance at all now. They had made their move. It was up to Martin to choose the path he would take. Marjan Boja was nothing other than a criminal to Martin. Nothing more. Now, he distinctly saw that his ties were far more complex than he had thought. This offer, in exchange for his release, made the situation far more thorny and complicated. The spider was spinning a broader and more intricate net. This was why Martin had not seen fit to speak further to Andi. Andi became involved involuntarily in this whole episode. He had become a naïve courier in this tricky situation.

Not even for one second did the thought of doing a deal with the Mafia cross his mind. That would never happen, no matter what the cost. Meanwhile, it occurred to him that they would apply the same form of corruption regarding the judges! They were out to get what they wanted, without a doubt. In the final account, the judges decide on Marjan Boja's sentencing or innocence. These thoughts troubled him. He felt the pessimism. What if this did happen for real? What then? The office furniture and paraphernalia swayed suddenly like swings in the playground. He struggled to pull himself together and calm down. It was impossible.

With bitterness, he felt himself snigger uncontrollably at the thought of 1.5 million euros. He recalled the many years it had taken him to pay off the fifty thousand Euro bank loan on his apartment and how he rejoiced like a child once it was done.   And now he was being offered millions by unidentified persons. Again, he could visualize these characters. He couldn't get the image of them out of his mind even though he wanted to dismiss it. Immaculately suited and booted in the attire of the most expensive brand names. The most elegant gait. Silent, of few words. Intense and probing in the way they looked at you. They are individuals who have never read a book cover to cover, who barely know how to write, but who manage to access everything and place it at their availability. Despite their sinister objectives, they distinguish themselves for outstanding instincts and gifts of intelligence. Daring, adventurous, and conscious that their entire paths through life are one colossal gamble. They've sacrificed everything in the ruthless thrust for instantaneous wealth and gear up to either win all or plummet into the abyss and end up in prison with the keys tossed into the sea. These are the individuals who offer millions to close one single case. The thought terrified him. In the final account, this was the business they ran. It is their vocation, but not his. They acknowledge their unwritten codes that function regardless of state boundaries. They don't refer to cross-state conventions, agreements, or treaties reached at the end of endless sittings. They abide by no Constitution or laws. They are nothing other than practical and instantaneous in their decision-making.

Lost in deep thought over this symbiosis and at loggerheads with himself, Martin unfolded the letter again without further ado and wrote the following note across the top: "To be verified and acted upon immediately." Beneath the lines addressing him directly, Martin described the circumstances of how this letter had reached him. He slipped a paper clip over the corner, placed it back in the white envelope, and filed it immediately in the top-secret protocol.

No matter what happened after this, there was a paper trail to initiate any further investigation. Martin couldn't bear having that letter in his possession any longer. The Special Operations Sector would immediately begin the verification of the owners of the company where Andi was employed and would find out about and document their ties with Marjan Boja. It would be a lengthy and complicated investigation. These millionaires who came from nothing were gradually working to make themselves legitimate. Their names would be registered at the Tax Office and in the systems of the state structures. Their goal was to relish now what they had sacrificed for - to become legal entities, all-powerful and robust. Marjan Boja's trial would not take long. Following the presentation of the indictment, the Defence presents its closing statements. In the final sitting, the Judge delivers the verdict. The investigation into this letter would get underway immediately, and who knows when it will end? This inquiry would trigger a far more complicated investigation than the current case of Marjan Boja.

Chapter V

The bullet of the traitor in the House of Justice to try and shake himself free, to some extent, of the living hell Arjana had plunged him into but also to persist with the "dialog" with his soulmate Artur, Martin got up and opened one of the drawers where he kept a copy of the file on Artur's murder. He weighed the file in his hands, a great sadness pervading his soul. He felt he was holding Artur's head in the palms of his hands, those plumpish cheeks, that short, fleeting life.

He recalled the day Investigator Arsen Gashi turned up at the office first thing in the morning, plonked himself down in his chair, dragged a file from his brown leather satchel, and slapped it on the desk. The name on the front cover of the thick cardboard file immediately caught Martin's eye, "Artur Rrasa." He felt the buzz. In his mind's eye, he pictured Turi sitting opposite him again, the way he fidgeted impatiently before opening a discussion, so energetic and eager to find out the latest evidence accumulated on different cases. The last thing Martin had ever thought was that the image of Artur would endure merely in lines of words filed away in dossiers and facsimiles. He held on to a copy of that dossier as a keepsake. The original had departed on its voyage. He remembered the day when Arsen had stormed into the office.

"Right, I'm here to analyze the file on Artur's murder.," Arsen stated, his eyes fixed on the file, which he opened and began leafing through.

"What's the latest on it, Arsen?"

"I've already drafted the report, including everything related to all our work and the latest expert reports sent through and administered."

They had been working on this case for months; the case of Artur's murder had become like a hot potato for Martin. They had cross-analyzed it together multiple times. Martin considered this a personal challenge and worked with great grit to solve this serious crime. Martin had these visions, like in a nightmare, where a ghostlike Artur would appear shouting with all his might, "Hey, somebody murdered me, can't you see that? I am dead. When will you revenge my death?"

"Arsen, I will sit down later on and read your report thoroughly," Martin said, looking him straight in the eye. Without drawing his breath, Martin became engrossed in the intricate details of the material.

"Martin, we know who it was; we have a suspect!"

"What do you mean, we know who it is? Martin exclaimed, jumping in his seat as if something stung him. "We know who it is?!

Such crucial information, and he knew nothing about it?

"Yes, in my opinion, he is fully exposed," Arsen said levelly as if relieved of a considerable burden. Bardhyl Mesi is our guy!" he said with finality.

"Bardhyl Mesi?!" Martin echoed the name. Suddenly, all his senses were alive as he strained to absorb everything. Instinctively, his hand rose as he felt the goosebumps on his skin. He knew Bardhyl Mesi. He assisted Artur in the interrogation rooms where Mesi was taken for questioning after his arrest on the charge of murder. He remembered that grim, dark, unshaven face, deeply furrowed and scarred. Martin felt the image cloud in his mind as his anger rose.

"The results came back from the forensics lab," Arsen continued, "which conclude that the strands of hair found at the crime scene belong to Bardhyl Mesi, confirmed by the DNA test. Additionally, the mobile phone company sent its official reply that the cell location of his phone on the day of the crime places him on the spot where Artur fell. Meanwhile, continuing to speak, Arsen kept leafing through documents that he shuffled around, reading only the experts' conclusions aloud. He then went on to say: "The reason for doing these forensic comparisons on this suspect was the case file on him that Artur was working on and the information sent in by the Prisons' Intelligence Service that during his incarceration, Bardhyl Mesi had repeatedly stated that he would take revenge against the investigator Artur Rrasa."

Martin followed attentively, fighting not to show his feelings of elation and despair. Listening to this conversation, he felt himself on another planet where Artur appeared to materialize in the shadows. When Arsen finished what he was saying, Martin was in no condition to discuss it further. The shadow of the deceased Artur and the image of the criminal who had executed him drained him of any thoughts.

"I agree, Arsen," Martin said. "I will also read the report you have prepared with great care, and then we can sit down to discuss details."

Arsen placed the dossier on the work table and departed. Left to his own devices, Martin stood up stiffly and began pacing the length and breadth of the not-so-large office. He glanced out the window. Spring and its beautiful vistas were in gradual withdrawal. He had not had the chance to enjoy or even think of this intoxicating season that had come and slipped away just like that. The intensity of the job and the actual workload had transformed Martin into a robot insensitive to what was happening around him. Scenarios of crimes, evidence, and case files rotated constantly in his mind. His routine, the days, nights, or seasons, had little relevance. His routine was an inaudible, tangled struggle. He battled it out with himself, focused on his goals and the success of his efforts and exertions, to which there seemed to be no end. And whenever he concluded, when he had hard evidence on an aspect of the case, his joy knew no bounds. This is about the only short-lived satisfaction the profession offers, nothing much else. Therefore, discovering the perpetrator who had murdered his friend was a kind of release.

So, Bardhyl Mesi was Artur's killer. Artur had arrested him. Martin remembered that only too well. He recalled how hard it had been for Artur to reach the point of Mesi's arrest. It took more than thirteen months of investigation. Martin had had his doubts about Bardhyl Messi; there was something about this individual that set off alarm bells in him, so much so that when Martin learned of the murder, the thought of Bardhyl Mesi had crossed his mind that he could well be one of the lead suspects. He couldn't remember whether he had shared these suspicions with Arsen.

In the horrific year of '97, Bardhyl Mesi was one of the key protagonists who laid down the law in the capital. He had accumulated a massive amount of money by murdering, plundering, and forcefully bribing some of the most influential business people of the time. The case files written on investigations carried out back then were superficial and incomplete. Anyway, most of these files were either burnt or stolen during that period of outright anarchy and the absence of the State. Artur had returned to the surviving files and started rummaging through them. It was risky entering this terrain. These criminals had committed severe, unthinkable crimes, they had grown more assertive with the massive amount of dirty money to back them, and they had laid the foundations of powerful ties with politics. One man of this caliber was Bardhyl Mesi.

Artur Rrasa had re-opened a suspended investigation into a case of the murder of a businessman in Tirana. The latter had refused to cough up the hefty fine Bardhyl Mesi had demanded of him. Witnesses had known of the circumstances and setbacks the businessman was experiencing before the incident, but somebody had silenced them, and they had refused to testify. Not even the family members of the businessman showed any sign of collaboration with the Police to help find out what had happened. Different business people went ahead and paid the bribes, and no one ratted on Bardhyl Mesi. These were insane times. There was no trust, and citizens felt intimidated. And they were right. By diligently studying these files, Artur had discovered documented evidence showing a pistol was found tossed into the nearby bushes very close to the spot where the murder had happened. At the outset of the inquiry, a fingerprint had been lifted from the cartridge of the weapon that was later discarded in the bushes. The forensics expert had ruled out the fingerprint as valid evidence.

Unfaltering in his suspicions, Artur had insisted on a new forensic examination of this print, but this time at a forensics laboratory outside the country. They waited weeks for the results. Finally, the reply arrived from abroad. The forensics dactyloscopy concluded that this fingerprint had retained identification values. Evidence had deliberately been tampered with in our crime laboratory. Artur had felt very disheartened by the corruption of our colleagues; however, on the other hand, the conclusion of the foreign experts was crucial to finally laying hands on the person who had committed this crime. Apart from this, the ballistic comparisons revealed fascinating findings. One cartridge, found and pinned to a spot beside the victim's vehicle, had been fired from the gun taken in as evidence on the day of the murder; the same weapon with the cartridge forensics had lifted the fingerprint from.

In other words, the link was forged between the killer, the weapon used in this crime, and the victim. In this situation, there was no longer a need for eyewitnesses, who, at the time, had no integrity anyway. They changed their testimonies from their original statements. Without a doubt, they were being coerced, and by the time the case came before a judge, everything would have changed in their stands.

The final report arrived sometime later. The conclusion was that the print on the cartridge of the murder weapon belonged to Bardhyl Mesi. For Artur, this was a huge relief. He had lost count of how often the case had plunged him into despair. Martin remembered they had discussed the case in the office, also bringing Arsen in to discuss the evidence.

Bardhyl Mesi was a notorious criminal of considerable experience. He had taken measures to prevent this murder from ever being solved. All threads linked him directly to influential politicians. He had bribed the forensics expert to modify the Expert's Report so that the print would appear invalid. This corrupt expert had got away with it scot-free.

When the warrant for the arrest of Bardhyl Mesi was issued, and he found himself in an interrogation room opposite Artur, Mesi had roared, cursed, and swore uncontrollably. He had never expected arrest and vehemently denied everything. He refused a lawyer, insisting he did not need a Defence Counsel. According to Mesi, everything brought against him had been manipulated. With the sort of political muscle Mesi enjoyed, he was considered untouchable. The only thing that had landed him rightfully where he belonged, behind bars, was the dogged persistence of Artur Rrasa. When confronted with the experts' reports, he had stared directly at Artur the whole time as if wanting to carve him into pieces and bury the remains. On several occasions, Artur took Martin to the interrogation sessions where they tried to get the truth out of Mesi. In these sessions, Martin came face to face with a being who had little to do with a human being. Bardhyl Mesi was a name that was familiar to Martin as one of the kingpins of crime in Tirana, but this was the first time he had seen him close up. To Martin, this person was a monster lacking basic civilized feelings. He resembled a wild animal, insane with hatred.

After months and months of interminable trial sittings, the Court, on the grounds of insufficient evidence, ruled the accusation of murder invalid. The Court upheld that there were far too many gaps in the evidence submitted. The accused was charged with illegal possession of firearms, and that was the extent of it. Artur's reaction and the scale of his demoralization were indescribable. Phony witnesses, produced and prepped by the defence, testified that the accused had not been near the crime scene on the day. The Court declared that the false testimonies appeared closer to the truth than the scientific expertise reflected in the experts' reports. The scientifically proven evidence failed to convince the court of Mesi's guilt. In a given sense, this signified an act of the State's capitulation to a bandit. Mesi's ties with people and the dirty money from his criminal racketeering lent him the strength and courage to take anyone on.

These were turbulent times when people felt insecure and profoundly disorientated. Justice was pitted against the damaged parties and the victims of unimaginably serious crimes. It was so painful; all faith in the justice system was crumbling and dissolving. From year to year, crime had mutated and bourgeoned with exceptional speed. Things had escalated from misdemeanours committed by the ordinary run of an offender in 1997, who, practically overnight, amassed fortunes, founded businesses, and consolidated ties with government officials, politicians, police officers, and judges. They operated with a great deal of prudence based on well-thought-through platforms. The result: no one lifted a finger against the judge who delivered a blatantly incorrect sentence or against the expert who manipulated the forensics report. Throughout this story, Artur Rrasa is the black sheep operating alone. He had rummaged around where it was taboo, prized open crime files that should never surface from archives again, along with the names of victims who could never testify.

Meanwhile, Martin, who remembered the vicissitudes of the case, recalled all the conversations around the threats Bardhyl Mesi had made from prison. They had failed to properly assess the importance of this information when they first received it. "It's quite common for criminals to make threats like this," Artur would say. But in fact, Bardhyl Mesi was different, and time demonstrated this. "There will always be bandits. All they do is mutate and re-emerge under different guises and forms," Artur had said at one stage.

"True, " Martin had replied, *"We have it all. The state and the anti-state, peace, and bullets. We are, as Father Gjergj Fishta once said, "precisely where our enemy wants us to be." Thinking out loud, Martin said that man invented the State to safeguard himself from his transgressions.* Martin felt he was a minute part of that State and Rule of Law. *Be well aware! It could happen again, whispered that voice inside him. Freedom always remains fragile and so easily endangered.*

Martin had immersed himself in his memories and was philosophizing about his past, which he had structured diligently, remaining a guardian of the law; it was as if he was talking to himself.

*No, that would never happen again. No way. We will combat crime and criminals day in and day out…*Looking up into the sunlight, he visualized Artur's smiling face and heard that familiar voice. *We will not let this happen again. Never, the Law and only the Law, not the street and crime.*

When they spoke about the Law and crime, about the fusion between politics and crime, which appeared to be well past the silkworm phase, Artur Rrasa would say about the exponents of organized crime, "They are aces, and they will overtake us via politics, and they will ambush us. They will slaughter us, but we must rise again, from the grave, if necessity dictates and never let them triumph. If they win, that will be on us, and we will be responsible, you and I, all of us…"

The man's passion was remarkable. To Martin, this passion was like a powerful propellor deep within Artur's soul. It kept him focused and fresh, like an eagle in flight. Standing in his office in the early hours of the morning, as if talking to Artur, now deceased, Martin said an emphatic "No. They won't win. Law and order, which we protect, will preside." No one mentioned him anymore. Only his memories remained.

Martin upheld that the atrocious year of 1997 was the incubation period of organized crime. Multiple statistics indicated that most young adults who had become criminals had lived their childhood during that period; every night, they had watched those news chronicles on television - "the inspiration for the future." That terrified him and he would recall and constantly echo the story of his past just as the church choir repeats the same songs and prayers every Sunday. He had made painstaking efforts to avoid any act that even slightly compromised him. He had veered away from many of his colleagues and friends, who had adopted the colours of the "political rainbow." He was aware of the fact that they were no longer his friends because it was the party, the circumstances, the power they wielded with all its machinations that made them implausible. Therefore, calmly and to their faces he had said, "You, there, me, here, and the Law divides us like a crossbar." Quite a few of them never understood Martin's withdrawal and his methodical home-to-office, office-to-home routine. He was never seen in the exclusive clubs or restaurants of Tirana which had now been transformed into a Western-type metropolis. *Do we stand a chance of winning?* That voice again from deep within him. He felt it was Artur's voice from the other side of the grave.

Reading the detailed report, Martin learned that Bardhyl Mesi had been in the vicinity of Artur's house on three consecutive days, obviously studying the crime scene. The identification cell of his mobile phone pinpointed him in the neighbourhood where Artur lived. There was no reason for him to frequent this zone as he did not live there, and from verifying statements of Mesi's acquaintances, there was no indication that there could have been a specific environment there that he may have visited before.

The evidence and arguments were all laid out in Arsen's report. The criminal who had shot Artur was indeed Bardhyl Mesi. The overview of this terrible incident was now clearly set out in the Investigation's File. Fact - that the inquiry into the charges brought against Bardhyl Mesi, when he had been arrested on suspicion of murder, had been carried out by Artur. Mesi's death threats against Artur were plainly documented and all of this had been reflected in reports from the prison authorities. Forensics results on the DNA accurately determined that the hair strands in the woollen balaclava, which Mesi had used as a mask when he accosted Artur, were incontestable evidence. These strands of hair had stuck to the inside of the balaclava which was found afterwards, a mere seventy meters away from the execution spot. Another very important detail was that the GPS of Bardhyl Mesi's mobile phone pinpointed him to the scene of the crime at the time the murder was committed. These facts and evidence spun an indissoluble web of the entire mechanism proving the suspect's guilt.

The case of the murder was taken over by Prosecutor Sokol Prroi. Martin was most satisfied with this fact, knowing that he was a dedicated professional. He had the habit of working closely with the investigators, further schooling them and giving them tips on the profession of investigation. Sokol Prroi was on the threshold of retirement after a long career and spotless track record. In this case, with the arguments he presented, Sokol convinced the Court to issue a warrant, in absentia, for Bardhyl Mesi. Police research revealed that Mesi had fled the country. Intelligence reports contained operational information, also recorded in the case file, that Bardhyl Mesi had close ties to the Head of the Fight Against Crime Department. This was a director who had ascended the career ladder with astonishing speed thanks to the extensive political support he enjoyed right up into the top echelons of power. Reports had also been registered regarding top-secret meetings this senior police official had had with the defendant Bardhyl Mesi. They had been spotted together in some of Tirana's most expensive restaurants and luxurious private clubs. On being notified of the inquiries against his friend, this Department Director informed Mesi of the charges brought against him and had helped him slip out of the country. Following the decision of arrest in absentia, procedures were immediately initiated for an international search. Although detailed information was regularly sent to Interpol, there was no concrete confirmation of his whereabouts.

Reading the data in the file and about the implication of senior officers who had aided and abetted exponents of crime such as Bardhyl Mesi, Martin felt sick to the core. When he thought that his colleague had been cut down in cold blood while performing his duty and senior officers of the Force were the tools of his assassin, the blind fury almost suffocated him. The faked expertise of the criminal expert also happened under the influence and protection of the top-ranking police official. While promoting his career, all due to political support, he trampled underfoot the corpse of Artur Rrasa. Any officer who had to work and investigate on the ground but, in the course of duty, interfered with these major interests risked the same fate.

Having said all that, the fact that this murder was finally solved was a relief for Martin. He frequently drove to the cemetery and laid a bunch of flowers on Turi's grave. He stood before the marble plaque and gazed down at his photograph embossed on the smooth surface of the stone. And yet, did it matter? Did it really have any value, the fact that the puzzle had been solved? The guilty party escaped anyway, went into hiding in another state, and possessed the money to have all charges against him dropped? The revenue from criminal activity at his disposal weighed far heavier than the life of a police officer. Artur could never come back. He was gone for good. He had gone, paying with his life for the security of others. So, what could Martin relate to that cold slab of marble headstone? It would never hear him; it would never return an answer.

These assassins seemed all the same to Martin. Victims don't speak; they have no voices to complain with or present arguments before judges. The only voice they had was the State Prosecutor. Martin Guri never forgot that.

Chapter VI
A forsaken illegitimate child

In the wake of the turbulence created after Andi delivered that letter to Martin, the latter gave his assistant strict instructions that he would not receive any civilian, not even those claiming family or friendly ties during work hours.

"From now on, I receive nobody except for official persons, understood?" were Martin's instructions to the secretary's office as well.

This was a "protective measure," primarily for questionable cases when individuals like Arjana deliberately use an appointment with the prosecutor to pass on messages of ill will. "Yesterday's "ultimatum" from Arjana and the "appealing" letter Andi had delivered were already almost more than Martin could handle. Both these events weighed very heavily. He knew that as the time drew closer to delivering closing arguments in the Marjan Boja case, the pressures and the blackmail would intensify. He half expected a call from "up top" from strictures of incriminated politics. Powerful traffickers, like Marjan Boja never moved without ties to influential politicians and corrupt Members of Parliament. *"One hand cleanses the other; both hands cleanse the face," Martin murmured pensively and added that these criminals secure the money to buy votes, and the politicians secure the criminals to buy justice. But not on my watch! I'll never allow this as long as the Law and morals are on my side.* It had been 24 hours since the meeting with Arjana, and neither side had budged from their positions. He did not intend to touch her son's case or take any action regarding a change in favour of a notorious criminal. But the question mark hovered on the other side of that invisible curtain: What was Arjana doing for her part, what move would she make? Did she know the bosses who had sent that letter to Martin? Had she told them the truth of what happened thirty years ago? Had she contacted any reporters yet? Had she contacted one of his colleagues who could then attack him officially? Would she write an open letter to the public to discredit Martin? He prayed she wouldn't.

If I resign, he thought, *if I reject this case and her son is released and walks out through those prison doors scot-free, what had happened would inevitably come to light. Even then, that would mean I am finished professionally and morally. What's more, the criminal, Marjan Boja, and his contacts could become life-threatening to myself and my children. No, I will stand with the Law. Or will the Law turn its back on me as happened with Artur and others who are left standing there waving useless pieces of paper while the judges release criminals before our very eyes?*

***

Only after meeting her again after around thirty years did Martin recall who Arjana was. Many moons ago, she had been a music teacher with the reputation of a woman who could cast a spell over any man with a pair of beautiful, glistening eyes that devoured you. In that distant province in the North, where she was living at the time with her family, people thought of her as a rose among the nettles.

For the young boys, Arjana was like the forbidden apple which no one could savour. Her grandmother, from the South, used to say, "Beautiful girls always look straight ahead." Before she married, she did exactly what her grandmother had taught her. When someone plucked up the courage to throw her an insult, they came face-to-face with her condescending and derisive arrogance. For her, vain pride was sufficient; she was proud of how she presented herself to the world.

At the city's Palace of Culture, where music concerts were often held, Arjana played select piano pieces and had been successful. When she finished playing, she would stand up daintily to thank the audience, bowing low, her hand over her heart. The applause was thunderous and unending. It was apparent that audiences loved the beauty of this woman; they seemed to devour her with their eyes.

Arjana completed higher studies at the Academy of Arts, and locally, it was generally thought that she would marry a composer or actor of renown. However, neither happened; all the bets made in the northern township dissolved like salt in water. Many assumed she would leave her township and move to Tirana, but this did not happen either. One fine day, the township was stunned to find out that one of the most beautiful young women of those years had ended up in a marriage to a man who had moved in from another remote district. At first, no one believed the rumours that Arjana had been seen at the Officer's House in the company of a young officer of the State Intelligence Service who had recently been transferred in. The younger men of the township were even quite shocked at this news. The whispers spread, "Well, what does that say about us, then?! Surely, we can't be that useless?!" "How come this stranger turns up and gets the cream of the crop, and he's a spook into the bargain?!"

She married the young Intelligence Officer posted to this northern township. The officer's name was Zambak Boja. Not too long after he took up duties, he had won the reputation in the township of an unfathomable and fearsome authority. Disturbing episodes had begun to circulate behind closed doors. For example, the case of Mevlud Buda, the young, much liked, and talented engineer at the local factory, who was arrested on his orders on charges of sabotage and anti-state propaganda. He also arrested Astrit Hasani, a teacher and poet. After Astrit had sent off a few poems by post to a literary magazine for publication, it was apparently found that the poems carried accentuated, decadent, and bourgeois content. The teacher waited in high anticipation and pleasure to see his poems published, but Zambak made him a gift of a pair of handcuffs and had him branded, "Enemy of the People and Party... Zambak had also apparently crushed a group of hostiles, who had allegedly sabotaged work on a farm on the outskirts of the township. This act of sabotage had something to do with the cultivation of wheat varieties. The competent organs maintained that with deliberate ill-intent this group had cultivated a variety of wheat, which, based on research, did not produce high crop yields. This was the buzz in the coffee shops of the township. The manager of the farm was arrested along with the chief agronomist, the Head of the district's Agricultural Sector as well as two agronomists employed at the Seeds Station. Working and plotting together, this group of people was the reason why targets in agricultural output were not fulfilled. This was hostile activity, but it had not escaped the vigilant eye of Zambak Boja.

These campaigns of arrests had won Zambak recognition and fame in the very first year he took up duties. In this case, he had become the shining example of the war the Arm of the State Sigurimi waged. His superiors in Tirana held him up as one of the finest examples of success, to be followed by other officers nationwide. For some time now, the township had been spared from further politically motivated arrests. The streets of the township almost resounded with the echo of handcuffs being clamped into place. Some mad man had been on the verge of pasting an anonymous poster up in the central square. On it, the simple question was written, "Why are you so cruel, Zambak Boja?" It was rumoured that the words were scrawled onto a piece of dark cardboard and had been ready to put up, but that someone had intervened and stopped it. "What are you doing? Do you want even more handcuffs?" this person had asked and had torn up the poster. After that, the township appeared to fall silent.

Arjana's marriage to Zambak Boja was one of the most bizarre items of news for the locals of this remote northern township. Zambak Boja had now become a person of importance. People looked at him with fear in their eyes. Everyone was suddenly on guard against everyone else. Everyone was wary of everyone else.

The barometer gauging the level of panic and fear was Zambak Boja. This person had found a way to penetrate Arjana's family and had managed to get their engagement officially announced. The wedding took place when Arjana was in her third year of university studies. It was ice-cold and formal, with select guests from the party and government—a wedding that resembled a party congress.

After her marriage to Zambak Boja, and on completing her studies, Arjana worked as a music teacher at a secondary school in the city. Every evening, the newlyweds would appear on the promenade in the middle of town and stroll up and down it a few times before sitting down at the coffee bar at the Tourism Hotel, which had the best restaurant and coffee bar in the town. They would then calmly retire to their apartment. The other evening strollers would look furtively in the direction of the young couple. They liked Arjana but were afraid of Zambak. The long shadow Zambak cast and the authority he wielded, caused feelings of anxiety. If he singled you out as an enemy of the party, you would end up in prison. Everyone was aware of this.

He was a man of average build, with a round face and thinning blond hair, which emphasized his broad forehead. His nose was slightly flattened and thick, and he had big, meaty lips. He had such a short neck that his head seemed to be attached directly to the trunk of his body. He had a peculiar gait because his legs seemed to join at his upper thighs. He always wore a grey suit, probably a part of the uniform the State provided. During the day, he always carried a dark brown patent leather case slung over his left shoulder by a long strap. This is where he stashed away the mysteries and the fate of people. He was always armed.

As time wore on, everyone noticed that the couple was not being blessed with children. Tongues wagged uncontrollably about Zambak's impotence. Others laid the blame on Arjana. They claimed she was barren and big-headed. One woman, mainly known for her tall stories, wasted no time in putting her frightening prognosis out there that Arjana had lost her virginity years earlier when she was still in secondary school, believe it or not. She claimed that Arjana had even fallen pregnant to the then music teacher and had had an abortion and that the abortion had rendered her incapable of falling pregnant again. This spiteful woman made these claims, but thankfully, no one believed her. Later on, not even she thought that she had made up such dreadful lies for this local beauty.

Some thought that because of the crimes Zambak had committed, God was punishing them. He was a sinner, a man cursed by the innocent people he had penalized. The curses of these families who had been persecuted would surely rain down on the head of this heartless human being.

The desire to have a child had begun to become a source of daily apprehension for Arjana. She was now sure that her husband was sterile. They never opened up about this subject with each other. Zambak was silent. Arjana had managed to say to him only once, "Still...but we will have our own child!" Zambak had taken those words in, in silence. He had glanced at her sideways and had not replied. No one could read his face, not even Arjana.

One day, he was to say to his wife, "Would you stop fretting about wanting children? The birth of a baby is simply a news flash. That's all it is! It is after that the problems start, worry, and sleepless nights. What if this child you have flees the country one day? Would we not curse that child? Didn't you see how an experience like this swept away the entire family of the Prime Minister?! Do you get it, Arjana? We are cool, you and I, and the world is afraid of us. Everyone is so envious of your beauty, and they hate me because I'm your husband." She hadn't said a word. "But, I am not known as Zambak Boja for nothing," he had screamed at Arjana at the end of this monologue.

Zambak Boja had been born pedantic, as such characters were called in those times. Incapable of any change in themselves. As far as Zambak Boja was concerned, love for the party and the leader was love for the Homeland, for the present and the future. An inner vow circulated within him just like the party used to circulate its internal flyers. He knew it wasn't Zambak, the person whom people were afraid of, but Zambak, the vigilant eyes and ears of the system in power. He got a kick out of seeing the other person suffer, like a moment of triumph over the pain this person experienced. These macabre circumstances gave him a sense of contentment. In the first years of their marriage, after the honeymooning period had passed, he expected the moment to come when this beautiful woman he had married would say, "We are expecting a child." The longer this moment delayed in coming, the more ruthless he became, at heart and in soul, to root out the enemy of the working class amongst larger families with multiple children. When writing his reports on these families, his hand jerked like someone with epilepsy. "You breed like rabbits, but we haven't got a single child, just one child, then I'll have an heir. That's the extent of it," he would growl and curse over his reports. When he wrote those lines about these families, to him, it was as if he exterminated their children, one by one, and this brought him endless satisfaction.

His gaze fixed on the black and white portrait on the office wall, he asked himself, "Why do you persecute only fertile males? Isn't that unfair targeting for personal reasons? How come you haven't arrested a married male who has no children? He felt relieved that he asked himself these questions and it was not his chief director, "What if, God forbid, the chief director did ask me these questions? How would I reply? The thought of it frightened him. He had to find a man who had failed to impregnate his wife. That is what his objective must be. Zambak Boja delved into the lists of names and numbers. He had no idea how to find someone in this township of V who was sterile. "Zambak, it is not the husband who gives birth, but the wife. The husband impregnates. The wife gives birth," said a voice that resounded like the decoded orders from the HQ.

He ran himself into the ground for several days in search of a couple in the town who had no children. To his great surprise, he did not find a single couple. One of his colleagues, whom he trusted, said, "In our town, we hit the target on night one. You won't find sterile women or men whose balls don't work in these parts..." At first, Zambak took this as an attack against his bad luck, but he changed his mind when his colleague added, "We even borrow a billy goat if the need arises," This local sarcasm drove him crazy. What was his colleague, a local, suggesting? The thought occurred to him that he could quickly put a bullet in his colleague's head and report it as suicide from a nervous breakdown, But, he couldn't bring himself to do it. Zambak recalled the saying, "Life is full of trouble; to each problem, there is no double." He checked on his side arm and left for home. "This time I will hit the target," he said to himself, almost kicking the door of the apartment in. He bellowed, "Zambak Boja is in the house." Arjana felt a shiver go down her spine as she lay in bed, waiting for him full of fear. She could never go to sleep before Zambak arrived home, that was an order and a penalty.

Wonder of wonders, just before the Berlin Wall came down, after many years of marriage, there was an addition of a son to their family. Arjana's pregnancy immediately caught the attention of the small town. Zambak was flabbergasted by this miracle. He was a staunch atheist, so he never thanked the Lord for anything; he did not believe that "fate was predetermined." Man makes his fate, even more so a man with revolutionary beliefs," Zambak Boja claimed. When his wife broke the news to him, not only did he find it impossible to rejoice, but he immediately began ferreting around to find out which one of his colleagues had knocked on the door of his flat when he had been away on special duty. The outline of a list of persons he could send into exile or arrest was forming in his mind.

During the initial months and years of the newly established democracy, the small town's population dwindled. Many young men and women emigrated. State-owned factories and enterprises were shut down and disbanded. The overthrow of the communist state shrunk and disfigured the small town, which had previously vibrated with youthful energy. The autocratic single-party system had collapsed. Zambak Boja was no longer the man who laid down the law in the toppled system. The new administration had sacked him. He had been shunted off to one side. People ignored him, although they were still not over their fear of him. Zambak turned his hand to business. He was among the first to go to Turkey and bring back supplies for several of the new traders who were setting up shop in the town. He found business as the way to become someone again. He wouldn't have power, but he would have money instead.

The day dawned when he was found brutally battered in the head and body with a steel rod and abandoned, left for dead. It was rumoured at the time that his attacker had been a former political prisoner. He had suffered severe fractures. He was found on the lawn of the town's park, a favourite haunt for couples who filled the coffee shops and bars until late in the evening. During the day, the benches lining the footpaths crisscrossing the park would fill with pensioners out for a stroll. This incident had occurred around dusk. The park's maintenance crew had found him at the crack of dawn the following morning, sprawled on the grass in a puddle of blood, unconscious. They called for an ambulance, and he was rushed to the hospital.

For weeks, there was no sign of him in the town. After leaving the hospital, he had locked himself away in his flat. Quite a while later, he was sometimes seen in the town's main coffee bar, but rarely. Then, the news spread that he had separated from Arjana and had left Albania. No one ever learned the real reason for this. Not even those close to Arjana knew the details of this unexpected separation.

Arjana continued to live in the town. Every day, she would go about her business. She was often seen in the town's central street, her little boy holding her hand. Although the vicissitudes of life may have begun to leave their mark on her beauty, she was still stunning. In those conditions, too, she preserved that dignified silhouette. Arjana continued to be one of the most attractive women in the province. She resembled the sun, peeping out and disappearing behind the clusters of clouds that graced her face. Men were hesitant to approach her because of their inbred fear of the shadow of her former husband. He was in the United States, but the shadow of fear recedes with a person's passing. It seemed that Arjana's ex-husband and her pride stood as her guardians.

***

The moment Zambak Boja began to make money from his dealings with Turkish traders, he siphoned off some of the money without telling Arjana. He was convinced that with the times that had arrived, money would be his most potent weapon to overcome the challenges ahead. He was a cold-blooded and ruthless calculator. In all his relations with old friends and new ones, his sole focus was the final goal, his gain. Every single new contact, every appointment or meeting, and every chat over coffee had a clearly defined purpose: what was there in it for him? Over many years, he had cultivated this approach with people in his previous, obnoxious profession. Schemes to take down people were his doctrine, studied at school and honed to perfection during his entire infamous career. He was trained for this, which explains why he was so skilled, convoluted, and complex. Distrust for anyone and everyone characterized him in every situation.

Apart from scouring the markets of Turkey for goods, Zambak also came across some ties in Tirana, and he began identifying customers who wanted to leave the country. Via a group of counterfeiters and contacts he had inside the airport police, he supplied these clients with fake paperwork and passports. He facilitated their getaway to states in Europe and the United States. The profit from this line of business was instantaneous. He was careful to surface as little as possible in the small northern township. Sometimes, he would run into people he had arrested and thrown into prison or exile as enemies of the party and people. He avoided them, turned around, or hid himself as best he could. These were much different times. The articles of the Penal Code based on which he had made arrests in the interests of the Party-State had been abolished. A new Penal Code was now in force.

The severe incident against him in the town's gardens had made him despise the place. He was reborn and enjoying another life. His aggressors had left him there for dead. A police inquiry was opened to find the offenders; Zambak Boja was questioned. He explained but could tell that no one was taking this investigation seriously. To avoid a second attempt on his life, he had decided, which, in his opinion, was well thought through and motivated in every aspect.

He felt entirely on his own. At this stage in his life, he had lost all interest in his wife and son, Marjani. Relations between them were ice cold. He had his reasons for this. This is why he was absent from their home for long spells at a time. The old town was like hell to him. Arjana said one day, "Why don't you look into us shifting to Tirana?" Zambak had given her a look of irritation, and without giving it a second thought, he had exploded into a fury of accusations, including marital disloyalty, claiming that Arjana had hidden the fact from him that the boy was not his.

"Tell me, who is the boy's father?" he had yelled at her. Arjana had frozen, this question being the furthest from her mind.

"What are you saying, Zambak," she had yelled back at him. "What is this rubbish? How can you say such things?"

Zambak had spewed everything out all at once. He was now well into executing his plan, which he had been turning over in his mind and fine-tuning for weeks. So, he cooled it, softened the tone of his voice and said:

"Arjana, I did not father that child. I know what I'm capable of and so do you. I have even done a DNA test, and the result is that another man fathered Marjan, and only you know who that was. If you do not want to reveal who the father is, then so be it, but do not stand in my way. I am leaving this apartment this evening, and from now on, you are no longer my wife, and Marjan is not my son!

He said it all, everything he had been wracking his brains for so long. He said it calmly with that penetrating stare of loathing. Without another word, he stood up, took a bag from the bedroom, obviously pre-packed, and headed off down the passageway to the outside door.

Arjana stood rock still, stunned. She felt the tears welling up, and she couldn't hold them back. Zambak never even turned his head for a last look at her. The door slammed shut behind him, and his steps in the stairwell were all she could hear.

From that night onwards, neither hide nor hair was seen of Zambak Boja, either in the little northern township or anywhere else, for that matter. Months later, Arjana found out that he had ended up in America. He never wrote again, and they never communicated again. The separation was final.

Martin Guri had just "dusted off" the story of Arjana Boja, a story that warranted a dossier of its own, it was not a criminal file, but it weighed a ton like the old dowry chests. Beneath this story, Zambak Borja had destroyed the lives of hundreds of free souls, including those of Arjana and her son.

Martin dragged himself back to the present. He sat in his office, at his desk, facing two large and complicated dossiers: one was on Marjan Boja, who faced the outcome of his adjudication and sentencing, and the other was an invisible file that weighed very heavily on his mind.

Chapter VII
Turning the pages of a criminal saga

Marjan Boja was getting comfortable in a restaurant east of "Piazza della Minerva" in the narrow alleyway of "Piazza di Santa Chiara."

On that January evening he was dining in the company of a couple, the same age as him.

He had just flown in on an "Aegean" Airline flight from Greece. A friend and his girlfriend had picked Marjan up at the airport. They had made a hotel reservation and all the other necessary arrangements as Marjan felt tired from the trip. They had headed up the internal wooden staircase to the left after walking the full length of the hall on the ground floor of the restaurant. They had reserved a table in the hall on the first floor, next to the window, from where they had a bird's eye view of the restaurant's entrance on the main street. You could watch the multitude of passers-by and different customers who visited this beautiful street lined with dozens of eateries with their welcoming tables spilling out into the alleyway. All the restaurants were bursting at the seams with clients, typical of Rome, perpetually teeming with tourists and forever magical.

They had just scoured the restaurant's menu and signaled to the waiter that they were ready to order when three men approached their table. Instantly, one of them pulled a badge out of his jacket pocket, while the other two drew their firearms with amazing speed pointing them at the three diners.

"Italian State Police," said the one holding the badge.

With no time to move, Marjan Boja and his companions froze in their seats, staring at the three plain-clothes police officers who now had the situation firmly under control. Without moving, Marjan Boja asked in faltering Italian, "What do you want from us? There must be some misunderstanding."

"We want you to carefully take out all identification papers and lay them on the table," ordered the officer with the badge. While pocketing the police ID, he waited to identify the persons at the table. Marjan Boja flipped his Albanian passport onto the table, while the man and woman with him had Italian ID. On seeing the documents, one of the officers spoke into the radio mic attached to the right-hand shoulder of his denim vest. It was impossible to pick up whether he gave a figure, a name, a coded name, or something else. Several other uniformed police officers appeared, who with no communication at all with the three persons, clapped the handcuffs on them and led them out. Two female police officers standing at the top of the internal wooden staircase of the restaurant took the girl who had been in the company of Boja and his friend. The waiters and customers in the restaurant, surprised but unruffled, looked down discretely at their plates or busied themselves with the menus and orders. Very rarely did anyone say or do anything at such moments. The plainclothes officers apologized, thanked the staff for their understanding, and followed their uniformed colleagues into the street where the police cars had parked, blocking the entrance to the restaurant.

About an hour later, Marjan Boja found himself in an office of the Italian Police providing explanations and answering endless questions. He was tired from his travels, but he was calm and collected, replied in a steady voice to the police officer interrogating him and looked him squarely in the eye. In this semi-dark office, the interrogator posed questions and fed the replies into a computer, not caring whether Boja's answers were convincing or not. Time and again, the officer gave him a fleeting glance but then turned back to tapping away on the keyboard as if he were filling out some routine form for an anonymous person of no importance whatsoever.

The Italian Police were simply executing a warrant for this arrest issued by the Albanian justice system authorities, who had informed them of the travel itinerary of Albanian citizen Marjan Boja.

The Greek state had not taken any action, even though they had had access to official information on Marjan Boja for several days. In the explanatory part of this decision, the police had fully understood the weight and danger this person posed. Accusations brought against him were grave. He was wanted on multiple counts of deliberate homicide, involvement in international drug trafficking, etc. He was extremely dangerous. Several episodes contained chronological explanations of crimes he was accused of, also brief, to-the-point summaries of the decision for his international arrest, issued in absentia.

The Italian police authorities had identified this individual at the airport on his arrival. They had not made a move at the border passport control, but police agents kept him under surveillance to see where he went in Rome and what contacts he had. They had identified the persons who picked him up, their vehicle, and the number plate. They had discovered that the friends were residents of Italy, perhaps relatives or just contacts. A check of the couple's bank accounts and activity did not produce any incriminating information. All this verification work had gone on while they were en-route. The number plate of the car the group was traveling was referred to. The agents were sure they would go to the hotel where Boja had booked a room, so they decided that it was there that they would intervene and arrest them. However, Marjani had not gone to the hotel but to the restaurant. Once the friends were seated, the agents judged this to be the moment to move on them. The police had now taken charge of the vehicle the trio had used to drive from the airport to the restaurant. After confiscating the keys, the police patrol officially impounded the vehicle parked in a nearby car park. It was a recently produced black Audi. They also found Marjan Boja's bag in it.

Meanwhile, other agents contacted the Carabinieri of the Financial Police and sifted through all their data banks for evidence of Boja's involvement in illicit activity within the Italian state. While waiting for the results of these searches, the suspect's fingerprints and DNA samples were taken. All standard procedures concerning such a highly dangerous person captured on their territory were adhered to.

All available information on him had now been accumulated. Three hours later, everything was ready to inform the Prison Police so that he could be held in a maximum-security facility while procedures were underway for his extradition to Albania. After verifying the circumstances and questioning them, the persons who had accompanied Marjan Boja were released, and their vehicle returned.

Marjan Boja was led out of the Police Station in handcuffs and bundled into an "Iveco" police van. Accompanied by two other police vehicles, the escort headed out of Rome. The detail was driving on the eastern side of this massive, sprawling city. Handcuffed in this cage, encircled by a metal netting inside the van, it was difficult for Marjan Boja to discern any objects as the vehicles sped past. About two and a half hours later, Boja understood they were in a built-up area because he could see the high-rise buildings, the streets, and pavements in the light projected by street lamps. After driving through the average-sized city, he understood that they had driven into the environs of a prison. He caught a glimpse of the sign above a huge gateway entrance the same height as the dense palisade of iron bars encircling the prison, which read, "Casa Circondariale L'Aquila."

After driving through the huge gateway and across a courtyard, the vehicles passed through a tunnel in the first building, probably the block of admin offices for the prison—another square and yet another building. The detail drove through a second tunnel in a building and pulled up in a small courtyard, fenced in on all sides by towering walls. Boja counted a total of eleven persons in the escort. With his hands cuffed in front of him, two agents grasped Boja by the elbows, helped him out of the van, and ushered him into a corridor, narrow but very clean.

Among the framed photographs hanging on the white walls, Boja noticed that one face, in particular, appeared at frequent intervals. This was the photograph of the famous Giovanni Falcone, the courageous Italian judge and prosecuting magistrate, mercilessly assassinated by the Mafia. Boja recognized that face because he had read a lot about him. At the end of the corridor, on the left-hand side, Boja was taken into a small, narrow office and seated in front of a dapper-looking, bronzed police officer with a trim beard, who asked him several questions and filled in a form with the data. They shifted him over to another office on the right-hand side of the corridor for a few minutes and then took him up a rubber-coated green metal staircase to the second floor, on the western side of the corridor. He was shown into a room to be his abode for the next few weeks. The handcuffs were removed, and he found himself alone. He heard the metal door slam shut and the heavy bolts clang into place. The cell was locked; he remained motionless, standing there in the middle of the cell.

He could not believe he had ended up behind bars in Italy; it was like something from the television series "La Piovra" (The Octopus) with Commissar Cattani. He smacked himself hard on the forehead, hoping that he would wake up and find it nothing but a nightmare. He felt the sharp pain, but his eyes bulged as he sombrely stared at the reinforced concrete ceiling and cold walls around him. He had ended up in prison?! "No way. It's all a bad dream," he said, mumbling. Being in prison itself came as no real surprise. Ever since he had chosen this path, he had been clear on the fact that only the bullet or handcuffs would be able to stop him. "Man is born for adventure. This is the adventure I chose, and it will end in glory!" Marjan Boja repeated to give himself courage.

Boja came into this world when the dictatorship was in the process of crumbling. The year 1997, when he was about ten, served as a criminal incubator for the younger generation. He grew up immersed in the world of films of war, violence, and killings. He witnessed the scenes on the television screen being played out in real life, throughout the streets of his country, in news broadcasts, and in the horrendous tales related by his friends. He had not read a single book. Glued to the cold, impersonal screen, he had become ice-cold in sentiment and emotions. He would laugh at people who got emotional and mock others who displayed happiness, joy, or wept. "People put on this great act; they pretend to want to, they pretend to feel sorry, they pretend to love. They are like me. There is no nerve or feeling. Violence is the only thing that brings people to their senses. After all, is it not sex that brings life, violence between two parties.?" He mulled these lines over in his mind, which he had read fleetingly in a magazine, and he felt that deep inside him, somewhere in his thoughts, a kind of logic existed. He had never given much thought to anything. He functioned like a robot or a wind-up toy of his childhood. Life was meaningless to him, or it only meant something when it was him doing the talking and acting when he was the only hero. The moment had arrived for him to be both hero and victim. He had always considered the Italians to be womanizers and allegro, but those thoughts changed when they clapped handcuffs on his wrists. "They're worse than the Greeks. I hate them now. I used to like them, but not anymore! When I get out, I will kill an Italian." It had been a black Friday that day in January 2019.

The cell, with its white-painted walls, had a metal bed fixed to the wall to the left, next to the door. The bed had a milky-coloured foam mattress and one pillow. Two neatly folded blankets were placed in the middle of the bed. Above the bedhead, fixed to the wall, the cell had a window secured by thick iron bars in the form of a square net.

On the outer side, you could see the finer metal netting, and then came the shutters like Venetian blinds, the slits of which had been adjusted so that the inmate could only see thin lines of sky. There was no hope of seeing anything below in the inner courtyard of the prison. Opposite the bed, the cell also had a small legless tabletop fixed to the wall with a plastic stool tucked away underneath. A small wooden shelf had been mounted on the wall to the right of the window. At the foot of the bed, on the opposite wall, a tiny television set sat, silent, on a wall mount, its screen behind a reinforced glass cover. The plastic remote control to flick through the censured channels lay alongside it. The small WC with its metal door was next to the entrance door of the cell. This cell and its amenities were all that was available to Marjan Boja. He had no idea how long he would be here. This was the first time he experienced the human sensation of being in prison for an undetermined period. To his surprise, he felt strangely at ease.

Marjan Boja was now a young man a little above thirty. When still young, his father, Zambak Boja, divorced his mother, Arjana Boja, and left the two of them for good. After several years of living together, they sold their house in the northern town and moved to the capital. After much effort, his mother found a simple apartment and returned to her vocation of teaching music. They had had a tough time of it.

When he was still a child, Marjan Boja felt guilty about being the son of a former Sigurimi officer employed by the Intelligence Service of the Albanian state during the dictatorship. People turned their backs on him with resentment and hatred during those years, just as people cursed and despised many other figures and defenders of that regime. Front row, in the group of the most detested, were the ones linked to the State Intelligence Service and the other organs of the dictatorship, those who had maltreated innocent citizens. The father of Marjan Boja had been one such individual. The figure of his father had become a nightmare for him.   His schoolmates tormented and plagued him mercilessly. "He's the son of that Sigurimi officer," he would hear the other children whisper behind his back.

One day, Marjan Boja beat up a young girl who dared to innocently laugh at him after being pointed at and provoked by a group of boys. He felt no pain or remorse as he hammered the girl. Quite the opposite, he laughed when he saw his fists had drawn blood from her cracked lips. He had a wild desire to watch that blood trickle. The sight of blood aroused a killer instinct in him.

With a superhuman effort, Marjan Boja completed ten years of schooling. He always hung out with boys older than him, some of the most rebellious teenagers in his neighborhood. His mother was in a perpetual state of worry and anxiety for him in the years that followed.

She was shocked when her son would bring a girl home and take her into his bedroom without the slightest care that his mother was in the house. When that happened, he ignored her completely. Her son's behaviour frightened Arjana Boja. She frequently fled from the house without any idea where she could go for the night. One day, she plucked up the courage to say, "Marjan dearest, don't do this. This is not life, pull yourself together and find a nice girl, one of the best, and marry." But he only snared and snapped back at her, brushing her off without any regard for what she said to him. Despite this, Arjana believed that one day, her son would get his life on track. Arjana hoped and dreamed the day would come.

When his son was born, Zambak had wanted to give him the name Ideal, but then he thought of Patriot for a name, or Vendim (Decision), Kongres (Congress), Stalin, or even

Enver; why not?! Arjana had been very clear that she didn't like these names. "No, none of those names. You will always be a communist, through and through," she had said to him while wracking her brain for a suitable name for her firstborn and her last. She would have no repeat adventures like the one in the silicate brick building. "No, never again. That was pure insanity, madness,"! Arjana repeated to herself like a chorus of a song. Only she knew what that insanity was. She used to say to herself, "Madness, Arjana. Craziness. What you did was outright lunacy."!

She was looking for a name so that every time she spoke it, the memory of the wild act she had committed in the grip of feral instincts and despair would come back to her. So that she didn't altogether wither and dry up genetically. "How could you do something so insane, Arjana!" She could feel the throbbing in her head, like the blood spurting from the ruptured placenta. Like someone trying to take revenge against oneself, she felt an inner hatred for everything. She hated Zambak. She hated her parents for finding her a husband of their choosing, her entire family who came to visit innumerable times when she fell pregnant, everything!

"Madness, madness, Arjana"! All her life, she fought both to forget but also to remember what had happened. But the inner voice, like that annoying next-door neighbour who forces you to change your neighborhood, is still in your head. "Mar (the root of the Albanian word for madness), plus my name, Arjana, makes Marjan!" That's it, Marjan! I will call my son, Marjan! Marjan is a name that bears the secret of life itself. Done it! Mummy's Marjan."

At first, Zambak liked the name when he heard it, but suddenly, he rejected it, "Marjan sounds too much like Matjan, you may as well call him Hamit Matjan (an active opponent of the communist regime, executed by the state in April 1954), Zambak screamed, "No, forget it, we can't have that," he had shouted at his wife back then. But Arjana was determined. To her, the names he chose were like those ogres that gobbled one another up. "So, what are you thinking, Violet, Rose?! I am not having it! The baby's name is Marjan, and that's that! She was adamant and refused to budge. She was ready to go to the Registrar's Office. She would register the baby's name herself. She couldn't care less that Zambak continued to mutter different names. She wanted to live her whole life with the unthinkable but indispensable act she had committed because of Zambak, whom she regarded as a shriveled, debilitated bush, leafless and seedless.

In his teenage years, Marjan made his mother's existence a living hell. He had been picked up by the police and taken in for questioning on several occasions, suspected of being involved in different misdemeanours. What saved him from being arrested and charged was his young age. Arjana tried to get through to her son and talk to him, but he had a cold and aloof nature. Her words went in one ear and out the other. "I'm going into business," he would say to his mother, "I will be rich one day, the richest. Trust me." She believed him unquestioningly. She expected all the joys and sorrows life could bring to come from her son. She had no one else to share her thoughts with. But, again, her mind would be focused on her son, the result of her adventure as a woman. But he remained the same. Detached, indifferent, and vicious, like the man she had married on paper.

***

Marjan Boja, arrested in Italy, knew only too well why they had locked him up. He was composed and as cold as ice. He had lost all feelings of compassion and warmth. He didn't regret a thing; he felt no grief for anything he had done or may have happened because of him. He was aware that on the other side of the Adriatic, a prosecutor or a bunch of prosecutors had "worked very thoroughly" on his file.

115

And, in fact, Martin Guri, still ensconced in his office, acutely feeling the pressure of deadly silence, was the prosecutor who had wrapped up the work on Marjan's file. On one of the facsimiles were the words, "Murder in the Bloc on 23 November 2018." Martin remembered this event clearly. He remembered when Detective Arsen Gashi phoned in the middle of the night. "There's been a murder, Prosecutor; I'm ringing from the scene in the Bloc," Arsen had informed him.

Of course, this was not the first telephone call that woke him up, disturbing the night's peace- and the ensuing day. Another murder, but something told him this one like no other. Chilled by this agonizing presentiment, he paused for a moment, allowing this news to sink in. He felt like someone who had just been stunned by a deafening peal of thunder and waited with bated breath for the subsequent terrifying electrical discharge. Was there a message behind these lightning bolts striking so very close, at the head of the bed, a place of peace and love?!

"Arsen, can you give me any more details?"

"I've just arrived on the scene," Arsen went on, "There is a body of a young male in a flat on the top floor of a building here. The victim was shot dead. He has not yet been identified."

Martin lowered his voice. His wife was sound asleep. She slept peacefully. "Like never before...," he recalled the words and Eliza's smiling face before she went to sleep. He tried to take the edge out of the information Arsen had given him because, in his life and job, he had often been woken up in the early hours of the morning by calls about tragic happenings that had become as routine as morning coffee.

"The murder took place roughly about thirty minutes ago," Arsen went on. "One of the neighbours who is being identified as we speak called the Operations Room."

In a few words that was everything he gave the Prosecutor.

"Please send me your exact location, and I'll be on my way. I'll see you there," Martin said, ending the call.

He felt empty in the pit of his stomach, and for the umpteenth time, he thought about the high level of risk his job carried. *It has everything to do with people's lives and their fate.* He thought of the work he had done as an investigator for the Judicial Police, the real passion for the job he had felt back then. Undoubtedly, his career had progressed well; he was now a prosecutor for grave crimes in the capital city. Investigations into so many cases had disorientated him slightly. The successes filled him with pride and fervour; failures made him despair for real.

He had a sturdy character and a keen sense of assessment in all circumstances, but crime, too, had become sophisticated. The saying, "The Devil flies with the wind," came to mind. News snippets came and went like the wind, but he was the one—the prosecutor who had to hunt down the killer, find the motivation, and assess the circumstances.

Everything remained suspended in the air in his job until he found the thread like the Lever of Archimedes, and then he could breathe more easily, although surrounded by scowling faces. Martin understood he no longer had the sensitivity he had had before, but he never wavered from his strong sense of professional and humane responsibility.

He got out of bed, showered quickly, threw some clothes on, and hurriedly left for the crime scene. His car roared up the incline from beneath the block of flats, and he headed off in the direction of "The Bloc," where the incident had happened. He lived in a suburb in the northern part of the capital. He contacted the Operations Room as soon as he left. To make sure, he gave instructions for the forensics and medical experts to be on the ground immediately. They should have already been alerted, as with every incident, but it had become a habit for Martin to issue such instructions in case of negligence. He could follow how instructions were being issued for roadblocks around the area and the exit routes from the capital on the police radio channels fitted into his car as well,

It was very dark, but Martin felt the biting cold of the night rather than the darkness. In a matter of hours, the dark would begin to disintegrate. It was late Autumn. Tirana was deserted at that hour, just after midnight. The only persons in sight were the street cleaners sweeping the footpaths of the main boulevard. The occasional car droned by, or a troubled drifter wandered listlessly along the empty streets. The neon street lights illuminated the sealed street surfaces a cold white. The trees still shed their Autumn foliage, and leaf-like runners stretched along the edge of the footpaths. Martin felt a twinge of sadness that Autumn would soon be gone. He loved the deep rusty red colours of the season and wished it could rule supreme forever. *Everything has a beginning and an end. Neither Autumn nor people are exceptions to the rule.* He realized he was muttering under his breath. He turned his mind back to the location of the crime scene. Turning right into the roundabout close to the stadium, he drove past the building, the Seat of the President of the Republic, towards the entrance to the Bloc where Arsen had said the incident had occurred. Turning right again, he spotted two police cars parked in front of the entrance to an apartment building. He parked his car and strode off in the same direction. The uniformed police saluted and pointed to the lifts. Stepping out on the eighth floor, he saw that one of the apartment doors was ajar. This is where it had happened.

Arsen ushered him through to the room where the victim had been found. Arsen and Martin had known each other for years, and they had worked together closely on many cases. In the lounge, the victim lay, stretched out, face down on the floor. He was a young male in his early thirties, tall, athletic build, short-cropped, blond hair, oblong face, and regular features. There was a noticeable dark bruise on the right side of the forehead. There were signs on his face that Rigor Mortis was already setting in. His hands were open, palms up on the floor. The killer had neglected to turn the victim over, face up, as custom calls for. The blood from the victim's body had spread over the carpet. Quite obviously, he had been shot at close range in the chest.

Martin was accustomed to being confronted by scenes like this, so he felt no emotion other than preoccupation to solve the mystery of every crime left in its wake. His brain worked to turn back time and build up a plausible version of what had happened earlier. Who was the victim? What did he represent? And the perpetrator, where may he have disappeared to? These and a series of enigmas seethed through his mind. There is an element of mystery to all incidents. And all cases have a reserved fate of their own.

Arsen identified the person who had notified the police, and he passed this information on to Martin. This person had declared that he had heard voices and then two muffled shots. He immediately phoned the police, but he did not see anything. Moreover, he had not left his apartment, which was next door to the apartment where the crime had been committed. Two police officers stood outside the apartment door; they had been the first to arrive on the scene and had taken up position there to secure the crime scene's integrity. There were two empty bullet shells a meter or so away from the body. Martin examined them carefully without touching them. The bullets had been fired from a handgun. The lounge was a mess.

On the table, in the western corner of the lounge, roughly two meters from where the victim lay, were two glasses, half full of a caramel-coloured liquid, possibly Fernet Branca or something similar. There was a small bowl of dried, roasted almonds and an ashtray with cigarette butts. The two half-full glasses indicated that the victim and the perpetrator knew each other and had been discussing something prior to the incident. The author of the crime must have been an acquaintance of the victim, perhaps invited by him. The victim may have been with a third person, possibly a female who, following the murder, may have fled the scene terrified straight after the murderer left. These were merely initial hunches. Martin's brain was now in overdrive. He asked experts who had just arrived on the scene to make sure they recorded every single detail. First off, the victim had to be identified.

The apartment, the scene of the crime, was modestly furnished. In the lounge were three burgundy armchairs grouped around a glass-top table; there was a small TV stand on which a "Samsung" TV set had been placed. Around the stand were glass shelves where trays, glasses, and several bottles of different, expensive drinks were arranged. There was not a single picture or photograph on the wall. And there were no books on the shelves. At the other end of the room was the L-shaped kitchen unit. Three plates, two spoons, and a cup, all dirty, had been left in the sink. The bathroom was quite big but messy; a bunch of soiled laundry had been tossed into a basket. There was a shower cabinet with glass doors and a washing machine. In the bedroom, only one side of the bed had been slept in. It was unmade, and the sheets and bedcover were soft and scrunchy. At first sight, the impression was that only one person lived in this flat.

There was nothing unusual about Martin being present on the scene. He was automatically notified of every grave incident. If he went to the scene, he would assess it or issue instructions on how the Judicial Police undertook the initial steps in the investigation. In this case, some mysterious power had propelled him to the scene of this crime scene. First, he had to scrutinize the scene and any evidence that could be found and begin constructing the mechanism of what had happened there. He had to build his versions of what had happened, check the reasoning of each one through and through, and tick them off carefully until the last one remained, the version that he believed would lead them toward solving the crime. And because the crime had been committed in one of the most upmarket neighbourhoods of the capital, it went without saying that the crime was serious, and the involvement of individuals would be difficult and complex.

The latest events and the cases he currently worked on remained unsolved. The manipulating and manoeuvring by the authors of these crimes within the context of these events were unbelievably complex, to the extent that their detective work yielded little hope for a solution. This aggravated the situation. All the available police officers in the Serious Crime Section had worked tirelessly for hours pouring over and processing data to cross reference information they had filed away in different dossiers, but no concrete conclusion was being reached. The latest killings were creating feelings of unease and panic in the community, while the media outlets kept pointing accusing fingers at the police and the prosecution. One investigative journalist, who had made damning and dangerous facts public about the trafficking of cocaine from Latin America to Albania, had been killed three months earlier. He had been shot dead in his car after leaving his home.

What was going on? What were the organs of the State doing to shed light on these outrageous events?! Newspapers front-paged articles with shocking titles gripping the attention of public opinion. The country's Opposition party screams blue murder with such atrocious claims as "The Mafia Holds Sway in the Country," "The Police are In on It," and "The Government and Crime run the Country Together," "The Government and Organized Crime are Exchanging Favours," "Justice is Corrupt."

This whole situation called for a reaction. Pressure increased after every incident. At the country's main seaport, several loads of cocaine were uncovered, but the organizers behind the shipment remained anonymous. Other shipments had arrived at the required destinations. Only a handful of drivers and peripheral business people were arrested. There was no sign of the bigwigs pulling the strings of this trafficking. Mind-blowing investments were being made, but the source of all this capital remained an enigma.

In this situation, Martin felt an entanglement of feelings and thoughts. Did he have the tenacity, or was he in the grips of a weakness that was bringing him down? He felt devoid of strength. He couldn't get his head around when, at what point, they would regain control of the situation and prevail over crime. In the years of his experience on the job, there had been similar moments, but they had been overcome with work, honest, by-the-book work, and powerful retaliation. Those times had gone down as their "golden times." He felt demoralized; he could not see the opening to how they could win supremacy over crime. That caused him acute pain.

On this fresh crime scene inside that apartment, Martin took Arsen aside and gave him particular instructions to make sure the experts assessed every item and detail and that absolutely every object was checked for fingerprints, including the lift. Everything else was routine, which the officers and experts did perfectly. Meanwhile, every bit of information was being collected to identify the victim.

Arsen informed Martin that the media was on the job and were already telling the public about the murder. Reporters had begun to comment on the event. The victim's identification was the first step; then there could be an official announcement of the killing.

The victim's name was Elvis Raja, the branch manager of one of the banks in the capital. He had rented out the apartment where his body was found. His home address was in a different suburb of Tirana. This complicated matters further. The murder and lack of sleep were taking their toll on Martin. After leaving the crime scene in the morning, he went home to rest for two or three hours. However, sleep evaded him.

This was not the first time. He had lost count of the super-overloaded workdays that began with a lack of rest and sleep and ended, often enough, collapsed over piles of dossiers and paperwork. The work he had longed so much to be involved in was becoming progressively more difficult because, in the country where Martin lived, crime was still looked upon as an affair with "extended family," "a friendship bond."

What he dreaded, along with every other detective and prosecutor, was not how the investigation would go or finding the perpetrator but who the "friend" would be who phoned him and would begin to spin the tale… "We look after our own, remember…He's in a really tight spot…We need your help…I'll never forget it for as long as I live… You'll see for yourself; do me this favor…" They were neither in-laws nor extended or immediate family. They worked in offices, with armchairs and teams of advisors, cabinet ministers, deputy ministers, Members of Parliament, advisors, local mayors, businessmen, and women. They spun a web that throttled every kind of professional effort, buried deep down every fact and shred of evidence together with the truth.

Not even the president…*How long can I resist*? he would frequently ask himself. *A little longer*…? It was tough, but he still didn't see it as impossible. "We must build a state that executes its laws and grows stronger with these laws by implementing them until there is no "extended family" left among us," a friend of Martin's, who has now emigrated to the US, once said to him.

On a study visit to the United States once, Martin learned that everything came down to rules, laws, and implementation. America was "report and register." And they say there were spies during communism?! No way. Real spying and informing go on in America. There, everything is reported and registered, and then the truth has a chance to be adjudicated based on the true sequence of events.

He had dreamed that Albania would be like this, "you see something, you report it, you phone it in…" But it was not as easy as it seemed. Here, the story is that within 24 hours, all assets are galvanized into action to find the "friend" and the "link" so that "the favour can be fulfilled." This is what made him sick to the stomach with his job.

With these thoughts going through his mind, he sipped his morning coffee in the office. His assistant informed him that Arsen had just arrived in the outer office.

"Tell him to come in," Martin ordered and Arsen appeared in the doorway immediately. It was clear to Martin that Arsen had not got a wink of sleep either.

"Good morning to you, Prosecutor."

"Arsen, good morning. Is there anything new on the case?" Martin asked, prompted more by habit than anything, as he knew that nothing major had changed for the last few hours.

Arsen stood up again, took his coat off, and hung it on the coat rack in the corner of the office entrance. Without uttering a word, he sat himself down, shaking his head despondently.

"Nothing!" He pondered things for a few moments and then said, "We have learned something about the victim. As I said to you on the phone, he directed the branch of a private bank. The flat where he was killed had been rented, and he was the only one who used it. The circle of individuals he socialized with have heavy police records. His name is Elvis Raja. We have reports that he is a close friend of Marjan Boja and Qatip Jashari, both of whom are known to us. These two spell trouble big time, and they are on police records as having a distinct tendency to commit grave crimes. We know the places where they hang out. Our agents are getting together further information concerning the victim."

The knock on the door and delivery of cups of coffee interrupted the report. The talk continued after a few slurps of coffee and deep dragging on cigarettes.

"The agents reported that around six months ago, the victim, Elvis Raja, registered a new company with the two police suspects I mentioned earlier as business partners.

Arsen failed to conceal his irritation as he spoke. He was obviously dissatisfied with what had been achieved so far.

"Do you have the paperwork on all this you are relating to me? Martin asked, scratching his head as always when he felt uneasy about something.

"It will all be in a dossier very soon," Arsen assured him.

"Do we know anything about the whereabouts of the victim's business partners?" Martin asked.

"No," Arsen replied. He pressed down on the palms of his hands by rubbing them together vigorously and added, "Marjan Boja has been tracked down to his apartment; that's his address, but our people only found the mother at home, and she gave no details at all as to where her son was. She claimed he never told her where he was going and frequently did not sleep at home. While the other business partner, Qatipi, was found this morning at his business premises. He owns a furniture shop near the railway station. He validated the business relationship with Elvis but said he knew nothing about what had happened to him. Full of skepticism and distrust for the person they were talking about, Arsen added, "At least this is what he told the officers who questioned him. I, for one, do not believe a word of it. They never speak the truth; it is deeply ingrained in their psyche to lie; it is second nature to them, and they are so accustomed to doing it."

They both fell silent. They were drained, and it was still early days to start weaving the thread of the sequence of events leading up to last night's murder. The information accumulated so far was not much. However, it appeared they were on fertile ground, and there was plenty to dig into.

Arsen left after they agreed to come together again the instant there was a development linked with the killing. Martin was alone again. It was 24 November. It was Saturday, a holiday. These turbulent events never allowed him the luxury of being able to relax with his family for the weekend. "Next week, next week..." He realized he had more than overdone the same old story with his wife and children with all his empty promises, but there was no other way around this...Duty to the State was a heavy burden that no one appreciated. Martin had the impression that the weight bore down only on the shoulders of the prosecutors, who were out there battling against crime and criminals every day.

***

In the first days of December, Martin, while reading the reports on the events of the day before, felt the tension mounting inside him. There had been another assassination attempt right slap bang in the middle of Tirana. The incident was appalling; it had happened in public, amid many unsuspecting passersby. The breaking news flashed across television screens, arousing terror and insecurity. It was thought that this assassination attempt was linked to previous cases. It had taken place in the morning close to the train station, a point of heavy foot traffic and many eyes to witness it. Someone had opened fire with an automatic weapon from a motorcycle against Qatip Jashari. He was sitting in the driver's seat of his car, which had been parked on the main street quite close to the Faculty of Natural Sciences. After firing directly at the driver, the assassin sped away into the alleyways of the neighbourhood, off the main drag, leaving the victim for dead. Police patrol cars were immediately notified and were on the scene within minutes. A few meters away from the vehicle where the attempted killing had happened, an elderly lady lay on the pavement, dead, and a child, who had been sitting there with her, had taken a bullet in the right shoulder. The victim had taken up a position on the pavement early that morning to sell some eggs, bunches of freshly grown spinach, a few tomatoes, and eggplant from her garden. Her 11-year-old grandson had been sitting beside her. His duty was to keep an eye out for the Municipal Police, who would confiscate their products if they were caught selling their produce on the street. This is how the old lady and young boy had been helping their family to survive. To squeeze the last dime possible out of her vegetables, the old lady would "set up shop" wherever she could, hopefully outside of the day's target range of the Municipal Police. If caught, her property would be confiscated, and she would unceremoniously be pushed out in an effort to keep the city clean. This had happened to the older woman several times, so she had brought her grandson along to keep watch. They would come into the city every day from a village not far outside the capital. Their worst enemies were the officers of the Municipal Police, who patrolled the streets to crack down precisely on this unlicensed activity. It never occurred to them that the bullets from rivals of organized crime gangs would cause a family tragedy.

The Police, the first to arrive on the scene, had rushed off in the direction the assassin had fled but had not found anyone. He had managed to escape. Not even his motorcycle was found.

Two ambulances rushed the seriously wounded Qatip Jashari, the child, and the victim, the older woman off to The Trauma Hospital. Qatipi was in no state to answer questions or provide explanations. He was hanging in there by a thread. He had lost a lot of blood from his wounds. The boy spoke, but he was in a state of shock. With tears streaming down his cheeks, he related what he remembered the best he could and kept asking about his grandmother. She had died immediately. There could have been so many other lives lost from that spraying of bullets. At that time, the pavements were full of people. The investigations group found twenty-two spent bullet casings fired from an automatic weapon spread out over the surface of the street and the pavement. The Police impounded the vehicle, a black BMW, Number Plate MM777AA, riddled with bullet holes. Half of the front windscreen and the window on the driver's side had been blown out by the bullets. The assassin had exited the scene, certain that with all the rounds fired, the target could not have survived. He showed no care about possible collateral damage. His sole aim was to wipe out the target. On the pavement about 7-8 meters away, you could see clumps of spinach and a few vegetables smeared with blood. Horrified and shocked, bystanders stared at the spot now courdoned off by the police, cursing and swearing at the government and the country where they lived. Police were questioning a handful of eyewitnesses. They explained the mechanism of the event, the features of the motorcycle that had no registration plate, and all that they could remember about the perpetrator. They stated that he was a young male; he wore a black puffer jacket, a black cap on his head, and dark sunglasses. This is what passersby who had witnessed the crime declared.

Qatip Jashari, the target, was in his early forties.' He ran a business but was on police records as being affiliated with crime. He had been arrested twice and charged with intimidation and extortion, but in both cases, he had been acquitted due to lack of evidence. Charges had been dropped in the course of the investigation. This was not an isolated incident in Tirana. It was barely ten days since the killing of Elvis Raja, and the police appeared to be disoriented, to say the least, incapable of clearly communicating what was going on. Insecurity was tangible right in the capital's center.

About two weeks on, the injured Qatip Jashar's life was no longer in danger. Arsen had gone to the hospital to question him about the attempt on his life. He had given vague and ill-defined explanations, no details of the assassin or a reason for this attack. Of course, Arsen understood that Jashari did not wish to assist in solving the incident. Knowing his activity and tendencies, Arsen understood that what Jashar planned was to solve the issue with the killer himself and not leave it to the State or the Police. Arsen was firmly convinced that Jashari knew the killer.

Martin was lost in his thoughts. He didn't feel just run down and tired but also alarmed when he thought about how things should be and how bad everything was going. From the Qatip Jashari case, Martin was now experiencing an illegal trend, a new ulcer. This trend of exacting retribution, of vendetta, was not only a very early practice but also an indication that the Law no longer had the strength to function.

Falling back on the Canon to perceive the Law was unmitigated evidence of this. The difficulty in enforcing the Law demonstrated the weakness of the State and its institutions. Execution, in compliance with Canon Law, visibly challenged the almost one-hundred-year-old State. The strength of the state setting an example should be visible in the enforcement of the law and not Articles of the Canon, which people have only heard about as a concept. They have no idea about its content or context, although it had regulated judicial relations inthe absence of a State for hundreds of years. Customary Law had long since been replaced. However, things were not functioning as they should, so the law became integral to people's social conduct.

The office weighed heavily on Martin Guri. There had been endless discussions with Arsen and other detectives, which had become draining and chaotic. Almost every day, they accumulated new details, frequently quite contradictory. The problems only mounted and became more complicated in the work for a breakthrough. Everything was read and re-read: dossiers, information reports, and confirmations, which ended up on his desk non-stop. The authors of the crimes continued their activities unfettered. Every day, Martin faced the desktops laden with paperwork and files with mounting frustration. They increased daily - the piles of memos and reports and the big, heavy files. Martin acutely felt the weight of being floored. He often felt like putting a match to everything and reducing it all to ashes. Of course, that was out of the question. He was an official of the State. He was merely having a moment of confusion and madness because of the exhaustion, powerlessness, and despair. He didn't know what to call himself, and the current situation. All he knew was he must come up with a solution.

The reports on the news reverberated in his head. To Arsen, on the other hand, it seemed as though he was working at a funeral agency, where they were constantly writing descriptions and registering details of victims so their bodies could be released to their families for burial. The criminals who committed these killings moved about undisturbed hunting down their next prey. Now, both Martin and Arsen waited for the subsequent murder. According to estimates, Marjan Boja was the next in line for execution. There was little doubt that this killing would come after the execution of Elvis Raja and the attempt to kill Qatip Jashar, two of his closest friends and associates. They had no clue or indication as to which individual or criminal group was settling accounts with them and could not determine which group Boja and company had scores to settle with. One of Boja's friends was now a thing of the past, and the other was still languishing in hospital. Bearing all this in mind, they believed it was only a matter of time before the ensuing killing.

***

Around ten days before Christmas, Prosecution was notified that a shipment of cocaine was due to arrive at the Port of Durrës. Foreign Anti-Narcotics Authorities informed us that this shipment had already been checked; its point of departure was Columbia, and its destination was Tirana. It was under their supervision as far as the Port. According to these Authorities, the key figure of this trafficked contingent was Marjan Boja. Finally, it looked as though the stars were aligning for the capture of Marjan Boja. However, there was no information as to where this person was. It was believed he was hiding out in Greece and organizing international drug trafficking on a vast scale. In his office, Martin called a meeting of the Anti-Narcotics Judicial Police Section and brought them up to speed on this important and top-secret information. The level of seriousness and professionalism with which this operation would be handled and its success would be of vital importance in strengthening the trust of the partners who had shared this exceptionally delicate information. They immediately set about drafting an operational plan, dividing up the operational units, and giving each group its tasks, so they were ready to go at the right moment.

On 20 December, around 19:00, early evening, the operational forces had taken up position close to hand and were following everything the border authorities were doing. The ferry had docked, and the work was already underway to process the many lorries rolling off onto the dock. Right on the mark, the agents honed in on the truck with the targeted number plate. They intervened and instructed the personnel of the Border Police and Customs to direct the truck with that number plate onto the Border Force freight scanner. There, they saw the quantity of cocaine in a container. The Border Police knew nothing about the information Anti-Narcotics had. The seizure of this shipment was good news. Later on that night, well after midnight, in his office, Martin organized the analysis of the whole action.

The cargo had arrived from Columba in a truck loaded with bananas. The traffickers had created space under the floor of a container to conceal no less than 230 kg of cocaine packed into heavily scotch-taped plastic bags. Anti-Narcotics detained the lorry driver who was there to pick up the container and the two partners of the banana company, recipients of the ordered banana shipment. The only missing piece was Marjan Boja.

The full report from the foreign authorities proved beyond doubt the activity and the role of Marjan Boja, who was the main person behind this trafficking. He was the most wanted person in every town and city. Every attempt to seize him had failed. The televised news spoke of the success of the cocaine haul.

In the heat of the intense work of those days, Forensics came up with a crucial find concerning the Elvis Raja murder, which proved that the killer of Elvis Raja was none other than his friend and partner, Marjan Boja.

This conclusion was entirely unexpected and staggering. They were not capable of finding the reason or motivation behind the execution. In all their calculations, motivation remained THE enigma. But, despite this, Martin and Arsen's feelings of joy and eagerness were obvious. They were now convinced that something had fundamentally upset the relations between Marjan and Elvis, but they had to dig deeper to uncover the reason. It would have taken a powerful motive for Marjan Boja to take such action. They analyzed and cross-referenced every fragment of evidence and information. Nothing was compelling.

There was an emptiness in his soul like a growing void, and Martin could feel it. The evidence he sought would fill in the blanks, bringing him a moment's respite and indulging his demanding nature without forgetting the woman at home whom he loved dearly and his two sons, who were the soul of his existence.

"Could I be losing as a person?" his inner voice asked, which only he could hear. He looked around furtively and heaved a sigh of relief when he understood he was talking to himself. Without hesitating, he left the office and headed home. He longed to embrace his wife, rest her head against his chest, and breathe in the familiar scent of his children.

A few days later, on a January afternoon, Arsen rang Martin asking for an urgent meeting.

"We have to get together; the sooner, the better," Arsen said without explaining further."

"I'm at home. Do you want to have a coffee somewhere? Martin asked, picking up the urgency in Arsen's voice.

"It would be better at your office," Arsen insisted, indicating that it had to be significant and serious. Less than forty minutes later, the two were in Martin's office.

"There's news, Prosecutor! Suddenly, our situation is far better," Arsen said to Martin, positively beaming with excitement. He could hardly wait to tell Martin everything and all at once. Knowing the way Arsen worked, Martin instantly demonstrated his mounting enthusiasm:

"What is it then, Arsen? Your eyes tell me you are the bearer of good news."

"I have just returned from the Trauma Hospital. I had a long talk with Qatip Jashari. I nudged him into talking a little about Marjan Boja. Well, I provoked him in connection with Boja. He's ready to work with us. He is willing to be a collaborator of Justice. He officially testified to the fact that it was Marjan Boja who attempted to kill him. Boja also killed Elvis. Everything ties up with the cocaine shipment we recently seized. Mobile phone analytics of the data generated by the phones they used has revealed another friend and neighbour of Marjan Boja, Astrit Duka. He was with Marjan the night of the murder. I have already dispatched agents to find him and bring him in. He will help us put together the events leading up to Elvis Raja's killing. Qatip Jashari had no trouble explaining the motivation behind it all," Arsen said almost all in one breath, bending down closer to Martin, illustrating his narrative with agitated gestures to make everything he revealed more grounded and convincing. He drew a deep breath and declared in a booming voice, "Bingo, Prosecutor, I do believe we have scored big time!" he laughed heartily.

"I believe we may have," said Martin, making no effort to suppress his enthusiasm. Smiling, he drew deeply on the perpetual cigarette always between his fingers.

"Start procedures for the arrest of Marjan Boja in absentia straight away," Martin said to Arsen. "I would think that he has fled the country on hearing about the seizure of the cocaine haul. So proclaiming that Boja is wanted internationally must be done asap. In my opinion, this immediate security measure is vital."

"Is there any latest information on Boja's whereabouts?" Marjan asked thoughtfully.

"Nothing certain. The fact that the news about the cocaine seizure is out there in the public domain now, without a doubt, sinks him. He knows that, so he will run for it whenever he can. His name is now appearing in the media. Information is being leaked from higher instances here, from the Police Department. Perhaps that's the way of getting the news to him. You know best, Prosecutor…whatever you say."

"No matter what, we will present all the materials we have in court tomorrow to make sure we get 'arrest in absentia' for him," Martin said in agreement to bring the conversation to a close.

Both men looked liberated from the situation that had kept them in bondage for months. They separated. It was late on Saturday night, but they truly felt a sense of relief at the results achieved. The invisible knot that had kept them entangled for so long had been undone. Lady Luck was smiling on them again. The public allegations and debates focused on the supremacy of crime would most likely dwindle and disappear once they had solid proof that would shed light on the shocking events that opened the front pages of newspapers and were the breaking news on the televised news editorials.

…All these different links in the chain of crimes committed by Marjan Boja had been painstakingly pieced together by Prosecutor Martin Boja and his colleagues, working day and night. Every time his eyes rested on Boja's file Martin would get a fresh take on all the pages in it and their content, including the transcribed mobile phone conversations and audio recordings made from a distance by technical operatives.

Chapter VIII
The risk of implosion

The four voluminous facsimiles comprising this criminal dossier were the weightiest and most important that Martin had ever held in his hands before. It had taken a vast amount of time, a great deal of correspondence, endless testimonies, investigation and examination minutes, confiscation decisions and minutes, and acts of expertise of all kinds, boards of photographic material, material sent by other states, boxes and boxes of transcription and so it goes on, to amass the thousands of pages of paperwork and documents. All this constituted the charges against the persons under investigation in this complex case.

This was one voluminous file that Martin wanted to get off his hands as soon as was humanely possible. He always experienced moments before presenting such files in Court where he would become lost in thought and reflection, philosophy and quotes, dreams, and paranormal situations. He always lived suspended somewhere between life and death, crime and life, fear and hope, but he never gave up. Should he be thinking of resigning?

Despairing, he picked up the heavy dossier again. It weighed the Earth…an image of his own funeral flashed like a lightning bolt past his mind's eye. "Where the hell did that come from," Martin asked himself. He jumped up and walked from one office to the next, jittery and apprehensive.

How heavy does the soil in the grave feel? Surely, it would weigh equally as heavily on anyone who dies? When expressing our condolences, why do we have the saying,

"May the soil be light for him/her?" Were Newton's Laws of Motion not equally applicable to all? What is the meaning of this Albanian insanity?

To Hell with it all! I will never feel the weight of that soil on me, anyway. I want to be cremated, and I do not want people muttering such idiotic death wishes.

On the day after Christmas Day, on Boxing Day, the Italian Police notified us that Marjan Boja had been arrested in Rome. He was deported forty days later. Under heavy guard, he was escorted to a top security prison and placed in isolation. Finally, he was at the disposal of Albanian Justice. Several rounds of questioning had already taken place, but he had rejected all accusations and refused to give any explanation regarding them. The investigation process continued for several months. The dossier now weighed as heavy as the red marble of Muhurri in Dibra. Strange, but he preferred this comparison to the earlier one, "It weighed the Earth." No one deserves to be compared to the Earth."

After evaluating whether everything achieved was beneficial to this investigation and that further investigatory work was not required, Martin decided to proceed with the final closing procedures and send the dossier for adjudication.

***

Martin had gone out to the interrogation rooms at the prison on that icy cold Winter's Day. He had completed interrogations in prison, with each of the suspects. Accompanied by an officer of the Judicial Police and in the presence of the lawyers of each suspect, he had contacted each one of the accused.

The most challenging of them was the key suspect - the most guileful and sadistic - Marjan Boja. Reports from the Prison Police said he had already installed his authority throughout the prison. Since he was extradited from Italy, he had been phlegmatic and blunt with every one. He was withdrawn and very tight-lipped. He rarely opened his mouth and spoke, but when he did, what he said was never disputed by the inmates.

Martin first came face to face with him in court when a decision on his detention was being made. He had just been extradited from Italy. The decision was communicated to him of arrest in prison, and that was that. Martin was to meet him up close and speak with him for a lengthy period during the contact on the completion of the investigation. He had put a host of questions to Marjan Boja regarding the final accusations, and Boja, with remarkable calm and that penetrating stare, had replied brusquely, directly, and defiantly.

"Go ahead and do your job. Write whatever you like in your little book," Boja said, an almost velvet tone in his voice. "I've committed no crime, and I reject every accusation," he had continued.

This is what every criminal declared, but different from the others, Martin felt that piercing stare. The accused looked intently at Martin like a tiger circling its prey, as if he was searching for something more. He stared for several long moments, not even blinking, his eyelashes flitting over the pupils of his eyes as if trying to stare the Prosecutor down. Martin Guri had tried his best to meet that stare, looking Boja straight in the eye, fearlessly, void of emotion, apart from the cold, impartial logic of the law that weighed down on Marjan Boja. Two pairs of eyes face to face, like the barrels of two tanks. Martin Guri would have liked to have defeated that odd, penetrating gaze, but despite the long resistance, his eyelashes quivered and surrendered, a kind of capitulation without warning, without the white flag. Marjan Boja's gaze didn't waver for a second.

His lawyer had tried to intervene, but the accused had shot him a chilling look and had said outright, "Your work is done as far as the investigation is concerned. We have nothing more to say. We have repeated this stand several times. That's all."

The lawyer didn't utter another word. Martin looked calmly at him, gathered up the documents related to the accused, and handed them to the lawyer.

"You may read them through again and sign off on them. Send me signed, official confirmation that you are acquainted with the investigation's final materials."

The lawyer took the documents and read through each page, handing them to Marjan, who sat in his chair without moving. "I read the minutes. I do not accept the accusations," and he calmly signed each page of the minutes and the decision. Martin was impressed with the writing of the accused; it was striking. It surprised him, but he made sure he did not express any of this reaction. He gazed down intently at the distinctive neatness with which Boja arranged letters when he wrote. In particular, he noticed the letters 'a, 'r,' and 'o.' The calligraphy had very particular visual extremities. Martin also had beautiful handwriting, but he could not get out of his mind the similarity between the way Boja wrote these letters and his handwriting. It was an authentic resemblance to his handwriting. It was as if Martin had written those letters and not the accused, Marjan Boja. If an expert were to do a scientific graphic analysis, he would, without doubt, conclude that those letters were in the handwriting of the Prosecutor and not of the accused. The delicate alignment of the roundedness with which Martin wrote these three letters in his handwriting was original, precisely the same as the handwriting of the accused when he signed off on the final minutes. What is this resemblance? Martin pondered deeply. He couldn't explain why this fact stuck in his mind. He threw another casual glance at the accused and found that he was experiencing a different reaction toward him. Deep down, he felt a softness, a vulnerability, compassion. Instantly, he came to his senses, making doubly sure nothing in his body language gave him away. After all, he was the Prosecutor and was doing his job.

The charges were very severe. He was facing a maximum sentence. Marjan Boja was aware of this but preserved his calm and clarity as if nothing had happened. After they had completed signing all the required documents, Martin turned to the officer of the Judicial Police who was accompanying him.

"I believe we have finished. Let's get all these materials back in order in the dossier, and we can leave."

Marjan Boja raised his hand slightly as if indicating he wished to ask a question. Martin looked at him and said: "Yes, did the accused wish to add something?"

He would have preferred not to pose that question, but judicial procedure required it. It was out of the question that Martin violated professional procedure, even though he was dying to get away from those eyes. That penetrating, ice-cold stare unnerved him. *He is a criminal; he has no compassion, and that's why he forgets to blink his eyes; he doesn't realize that the blinking of eyelashes denotes life,* ...the prosecutor thought. When he spoke, Boja's voice was flat and metallic:

"If possible, honoured Prosecutor, I want to know how long I will be kept here in this prison. I am innocent, and you, taking me to trial is pointless."

He lowered his head for a second but then addressed him again:

"There is never an end to all your procedures. Don't forget that I have been in isolation for months, in Italy and here, nothing but protracted delay after delay. My lawyers serve no purpose; they're useless. All they're doing is telling me lies...I feel you are lying to me, too, and you're probably in league with my lawyers, whom I have paid as much as they've wanted.

In the meantime, his lawyer had stood up, standing beside him. He lowered his head and did not utter one word as if absent. Martin glanced sideways at the accused and then stared down at the tabletop. Those uniquely written letters flashed through his mind. Martin noted that Boja's eyelashes seemed to be frozen again. They did not blink, and this seemed to distend the pupils of those eyes that had witnessed so many crimes, killings, robberies, and victims of drug overdoses... Martin tried to avoid direct eye contact. He had no connection at all to this son of a Sigurimi officer of the times of the communist regime, who now enjoyed freedom in America. *The bitter irony of a person's fate! I lose sleep over one of their offspring, who, despite their power, never paused to ask if their people had any food on the table...This boy's father enjoys America while I lose my sight slogging over his son's dossier. That is so unfair. Is this what we all fought for to bring in democracy?!...*

Meanwhile, the Judicial Police officer accompanying Martin was busy writing something in the dossier's documents lying open on the immovable table, informing the accused and his lawyer of the different acts.

"If what you say is true, I am in no way swayed to believe you or to say you are right. The file will soon be in Court. They, that is, the body of judges, will decide if you are right or we, who bring these charges against you in the name of the State, are right," Martin replied equally as calmly.

"Prosecutor!" the accused started up again when he saw Martin pull away to leave.

"I have one final request, if I may..."

"Yes, the accused may speak," Martin said without looking in his direction at all.

"Please allow a meeting with my mother. I have not seen her for months, not once since I was arrested. She is all I have in this world; I have no one else."

In mid-stride heading for the door, Martin stopped and turned back once again. He was struck by the resonance of the prisoner's voice, and he turned around to look him in the eye. He saw that those ice-cold, blood-curdling eyes of a few moments earlier were welling up with tears. The pupils of his eyes now shone through the tears. For a split second, he seemed human. It was as if he was begging his hand over his heart in anticipation of Martin's reply. That wall of arrogance he threw up seemed to have dissipated entirely. He believed him; the only time Martin believed the accused was sincere. The thought of his beloved mother, now deceased, came to mind. One always softens when thinking of one's mother. In that instant, even this man in front of him, a hardcore criminal of every dimension, seemed human. Love for one's mother and tears speak volumes for a man. Marjan Boja stood before him, his eyes full of tears, saying he wanted to see his mother. Without giving it further thought, Martin looked at him and replied,

"All right, seeing we have concluded the investigation, we will arrange a meeting very soon. I will authorize this with the prison authorities today.

"I can't thank you enough," Marjan Boja said, his voice quivering with emotion. It seemed like someone else's voice. How could the same vocal cords produce the defiant and arrogantly obstinate voice of a few minutes earlier and now this tear-jerking, "I can't thank you enough" voice? That last sentence, his tear-filled eyes, and the letters of his handwriting lingered in Martin's thoughts. Those eyes were deep-set, and they shone brightly. He had lost some colour and was pale, having not seen the sun for months. He had short, straight, black hair, carefully combed to one side. He didn't seem to be all that tall, but he was well-built. After giving him a last look, the prosecutor and the officer departed without another word, leaving behind them in that cold interrogation room, Marjan Boja and his Defence Counsel.

There was only one thing left to do: arrange all the contents of that dossier in proper order, ready for him to present in Court.

***

When he came face to face with Marjan Boja in prison a few weeks before his mother, Arjana Boja, barged into Martin's office with her intimidating message, Prosecutor Martin Guri could never have imagined the unfathomable character who sat across the desk from him. Not in his wildest dreams could he have thought there may be a link with this person, whether close or distant. Even less so could he have imagined that Marjan Boja would make him face the dilemma of putting his whole career and life on the line! Now, he could not get Arjana out of his head, plus the powerful "ties" Marjan had outside, who were making every effort to buy him off; they all lurked menacingly like terrifying shadows.

In this state of unthinkable stress on the day before the trial, Martin was thinking back all those years ago to that old story that had to do with the woman he had met one day earlier. This episode had been deleted from his memory altogether. The only time he had brought it up was when he had told the story to a childhood friend as if it had been a dream, and that was it!

"…I was barely 17 years old. It happened the year father was transferred to a township in the North. As an officer in the Armed Forces, my father and the family were used to moving."

"We were lucky. When we arrived, our apartment in a red silicate brick block of flats was ready to be moved into. It was in the center of the town. I was in secondary school back then. I don't remember why, but school lessons began at midday. I was at home alone, my parents were at work, and my younger sister was at school. A couple lived opposite our flat on the third floor. They did not have children. The husband was an officer of the State Security Service, and she was a music teacher. I don't know why she hadn't been going to work for several days. She stayed indoors all day and

142

played the piano. Her name was Arjana. She was breathtakingly beautiful, in her early thirties. She threw me some strange looks when we ran into each other. We had very little to do with the neighbours. That was a policy of my father to keep everyone at a distance, including the neighbours and especially the Sigurimi officer. He was right about that. Even my mother was cool and detached in any neighbourly dealings with them. When we did not invite them over, neither did they invite us. It seemed we had similar principles. Everybody was on guard against everybody else.

On that day, I was in the middle of doing chemistry homework. It was ten in the morning. There was a knock on the door. I didn't open it. My parents were very forceful about this: "Never open the door to anyone except us." Then, the bell rang. Curiosity got the better of me. I looked through the peephole. It was Arjana, the neighbour opposite us. I wondered what it was she wanted. I was silent. I thought I should ring my father and ask him, but that seemed childish. I regarded myself to be a man. I had another look. She was still hovering. She rapped lightly on the door again. Then, in a low, soft voice, she said, "Martin, please open the door…I only want to ask you a simple question." I opened the door. And it was as if she assaulted my senses with a fragrance of lavender which I had never experienced before. I asked her what she wanted. She didn't say anything. She looked deep into my eyes, long and hard. It was blinding that look, like the light of the sun. "How can I help you, Aunty?" I asked. Again, she did not reply. She continued to look at me. I felt embarrassed and could not hold that gaze; I looked down at the floor. Then she spoke: "Would you like to listen to a fragment of Beethoven on the piano? Do you like music?" Without waiting for my answer, she threw her arm around my neck, her long black hair brushing against my cheek. That lavender scent was intoxicating. She drew me over to her flat after lightly pulling the door of our flat shut. Good job the key was hanging on a cord around my neck otherwise I wouldn't have been able to get back in.

Theirs was a beautiful apartment. There were artificial flowers I had never seen, a few large armchairs, dark burgundy in colour. She sat me down next to the piano while she sat at the keyboard and began to play. She played beautifully. Then, pulling me nearer to her, she offered to teach me how to play. She took my fingers in hers, leaning over me. I felt her press me tightly against her body. I became aware of her rapid breathing; it had a rhythmic, musical sound. Never before had I experienced anything like this. I had never imagined a woman's embrace could be so warm. Suddenly, her breasts were being thrust in my face. I almost suffocated. Perhaps for a fleeting moment, I even thought suffocating in this way would not be such a bad thing.

"It's just a game," she said. "Do you enjoy playing games?"

In an instant, she had broken away from me and walked over to the door. After checking that the door was locked, she returned to sit beside me. "Play something yourself," she said, "just bang away on the keys."

My fingers wandered aimlessly over the keyboard. She stood up and pulled me in the direction of the bedroom.

"Come, let's play together," she said. "Let's get into bed and play. Come on, there's no one here."

In a flash, she had undressed. I could feel my face and my whole body going red with embarrassment and shock. She began taking my clothes off, and when I stood there, stark naked, she swept me in under the bed covers. I felt her fingers feeling, groping, and caressing my penis. Satisfied that I was hard enough for her, she opened her legs, and in a guttural voice, she said,

"Come on then, it's fun; it's nothing to be ashamed of."

I hesitated. I even tried to flee, but there was no escaping her. "Don't be shy, don't be shy… Come on then, it's fun.

You'll see, and you'll say I was right..." After that, I don't remember a thing.

I lost my virginity to that woman, and she was also married. It was like living in a bad or beautiful dream. Honestly, I don't know. This was my first encounter with sex, and I was still not eighteen years of age. Sex with a married woman! I didn't want to see her ever again. But she came back, every day at the same time, wearing the same intoxicating scent of lavender, and just like the Sirens of Ulysses she lured me over the passageway into her apartment.

This mind-numbing game persevered for two whole weeks. To this day, I have no idea how I managed to control myself in front of my parents, but somehow, I did. This two-week clandestine adventure could never be undone. It had happened. Then, she knocked no more. I was curious to know what had transpired. I certainly did not dare to ask her. I deliberately appeared in front of her a couple of times so she could perhaps tell me. She didn't speak to me. She pretended not to know me, as if she had never seen me before. I waited ages for her to knock on our door again, but she never did. She also avoided me.

I saw her one day. She had put some weight on. She was pregnant. I was numb with terror. What if she said that she had fallen pregnant with me? I was at my wit's end. Everything was spinning out of control for me. I started getting poor marks at school. A classmate of mine, Maria, who I was sweet on, would look at me in bewilderment. Surprisingly, I no longer felt attracted to her. I developed a cough. I was not well at all. This gave me the idea to tell my father that the climate in this area was not good for me. I was almost entirely convinced that I had got that woman pregnant. I wanted to get out of there as soon as possible and as far away as possible. To make the situation more alarming. I got the ambulance out several times and ended up in hospital as a result. However, they kept sending me home, saying they could find nothing wrong with me. Finally, Father was convinced and started calling in favours for a transfer. It didn't take long before we had shifted out of there. Ever since then, I had never set eyes on this woman.

This is the extent of the story with that woman who had walked into his office after thirty years. It was all true, but, brought to the surface again, in Martin's current circumstances, this story would be catastrophic for him and his family. Arjana had disclosed everything. She told him about the divorce, how much she had suffered, her boy, and the hardships she had endured to raise him, the wrong path he had chosen in life until the moment he had finished up in prison. She wept the whole time. Desperate and defeated by her bad luck in life, she had thrown open the floodgates and released the burning, self-consuming anguish she had bottled up inside for so long and literally spewed it all into Martin's lap. Shocked beyond belief and utterly at a loss for words, all Martin had managed to do was stumble out into his assistant's office, inform her the meeting was over, and instruct her to accompany the lady out of the building. He felt exactly like he had the day she pulled him into her bed - morally violated.

Lying in front of Martin Guri was the dossier containing evidence he believed corroborated the charges against Marjan Boja. Martin was scheduled to present this evidence to the Court on the morrow. Not to be neglected was also Marjana's ultimatum. The threads of connection with the criminal Marjan Boja resembled those fine wires on homemade bombs concocted by terrorists: if you cut the wrong wire, it explodes. He had seen several video clips with the bomb disposal experts, sweat pouring off them as they worked to disable tele-commanded explosives. Their dilemma as to which wire they snipped was not dissimilar to the predicament Martin found himself in. In his mind, the instant he had read it, he had snipped clean through the threads woven by the "Big Boys" behind that compromising letter "couriered" to his office. Now, he had to decide which of the wires had to be severed in the bomb Marjana had tossed into his lap: the threads that link him with Marjan, or the threads that link him to the Law?

Until 11:00 a.m. the next day, when he was to present the evidence, he had a few hours to consider what action he should take.

Minutes before leaving the office, he placed his hand on the dossier of the Marjan Boja case. Almost like he was taking an oath, Martin slammed the palm of his right hand down on the cover and said in a loud voice, "Here lies the evidence! Here lies the truth!" And he walked out.

Chapter IX
"Presentation of the Indictment before the Law

All through the drafting of his presentation of the evidence, Martin Guri had silently endured the protracted battles waged at every sitting of the case's judicial examination. These battles ran past his mind's eye like frames of a film, all the fighting and debates between witnesses and the defiance and arrogance of the accused, Marjan Boja. Every time he came across the defendant's name, in every accusation, Martin visualized those unbelievably ice-cold eyes. The eyes of a serpent or a killer shark were suddenly the eyes of a hawk and, at other times, of an insignificant fly, almost non-existent. At times, they were the invisible eyes of an insect, camouflaged, inexistent. Martin was surprised and slightly worried by this oscillation. He had never experienced this before with any other defendant. *Perhaps because he is the arch-criminal, the head of every crime,* he would think, and once again, when his eyes lashes dropped heavily over the indictment written in such beautiful handwriting, those unblinking eyes would come at him again, as if from the depths of the ocean, like two projectors. The eyes of this defendant, their iciness with every statement or denial, were like two waves colliding head-on to create the latest tsunami in court. This was, by far, not the first time a case that was such a hot potato had fallen into his hands and neither would it be the last. He failed dismally to devise a reason for this almost nuclear resonance that vacillated inside him every time his eyes met those of the defendant Marjan Boja. A puzzling coincidence or a coincidental puzzle? An answer or an explanation completely escaped him, a logic that would give him a reprieve in this unending analytical slog to accumulate facts and evidence and uncover the reasoning behind them. He would pause and read out aloud given paragraphs of the conclusions; with great care, he read and re-read the direct statements made by the collaborator of justice, Qatip Jashari, and the testimonies of the other witnesses, but, no matter how hard he tried he could not forget that glacial portrait of the defendant, that cold, disdainful look, his emotionless self-control, and frosty aloofness, the blunt negation, and detachment he showed at every session. This unorthodox defendant, never before experienced in the many years of Martin's career, could penetrate the mind and silently intimidate anyone who sat opposite him, including the prosecutor and the judges.

*This will be the trial of the year,…*Martin murmured to himself. He recalled the "Trials of the Bloc" (of former communist officials who resided in a top-security zone of Tirana, commonly known as "The Bloc.). They got underway amidst a great deal of flurry and impetus, with very high expectancy levels among the public and prosecutors, but which petered out into "trials over cups of coffee and black Chinese tea." He smirked bitterly. An instant later, he was growling at himself: *"No way. This is the presentation of my case; this impeachment is mine. This will be a court trial where crime will quiver in its boots, and the law will be executed to the letter. And the big bosses who sent him that letter will feel the weight of it. Then they can do whatever they want."*

Like all the other presentations of indictments Martin had submitted before the Judge's Bench, he began this presentation in the same way:

"Honoured members of the Judge's Bench.

It is my privilege and responsibility to represent the indictment on behalf of the Republic of Albania and to present the completed discourse related to criminal prosecution against the defendant, Marjan Boja, charged with…"

After listing the charges and the significant level of danger to the public these serious crimes posed, Martin focused at length on the risk the defendant himself presented as an individual with accentuated criminal tendencies against the State and society. He had not hesitated to describe, and he intended to state clearly to the Bench that if the accused were acquitted, he would never cease to organize further, even more dangerous acts to the detriment of the society wherever he lived. Martin's attention was drawn to another paragraph of the indictment:"

"…Moreover, the circumstances and facts submitted to this honourable Court reveal that apart from being the mastermind behind a drug trafficking ring, he also prepared, down to the last detail, and implemented with precision, his premeditated schemes to murder his closest associates in crime, his friends, without even sparing the innocent, to achieve his criminal goals, to reap in full for himself all profits won from illicit dealings, which ran into millions of euros."

When Martin Guri got down to the murky details of the crimes the defendant was accused of, he showed how the euros circulated like the red cells in the bloodstream, and just as they keep mammals alive, they also keep crime alive. No act, no assault against the law, or public life ever happened without money, euros, or dollars circulating. Crime and money bind like an inextricable alloy, like "another world." He, the prosecutor, that is, tried to wrestle his way into this "other world," but he suffered a kind of suffocation that quite frequently stopped him in his tracks, and he had to pause and calm down or retire to the balcony for a breath of fresh air. Every time Martin plunged himself into this kind of interpretation, he always emerged worn out.

Why on earth did man invent money? What do we need money for when it is the red blood cells of every human crime? Would crime exist if money didn't exist? He posed the question and paused. Money and man are like the Universe, which only expands, and its end is unfathomable. He thought of the cursed letter, directly linked to money…to millions of euros to buy the acquittal of a criminal… Weary-eyed, he went back to make the final corrections to the most important document of this trial.

Throughout the pages of this indictment, all the evidence was laid out in order, and the respective arguments validating this evidence that had been collected via official correspondence and letters of request of law enforcement agencies of a host of foreign countries on the territories of which Marjan Boja had expanded his criminal activity. It had taken a great deal of time for Martin to process all this information and then to arrange it in order, in line with the strategy he had drafted at the outset. By presenting the indictment before the bench of judges in a periodical manner, calmly and responsibly, with resolve and insight, the arguments would be lethal for the defendant, who did nothing other than follow in silence and deny everything.

"…Based on processed data acquired via information exchanges with intelligence services and international police investigations, special investigation methods were authorized, and a controlled hand-over was applied together with recorded conversations and communications. Everything is transcribed and can be found in the voluminous files and facsimiles in front of you, Judges on the Bench, allow me to present them, one by one…"

Continuing to read further on, Martin felt some relief. He had been careful when writing the indictment to unfurl the entire mechanism used to traffic the contingent of cocaine all the way from Columbia to Albania, the communications made, itineraries, collaborators, all implications to the most peripheral. He had also listed, backed by arguments, all bank transactions inside and outside the country. The letters of request from other countries left no room for doubt, but neither did they give the defendant any legitimate reason to allude to possible support for his systematic denial of the fake charges.

"…In the investigative procedure, information on banking activity related to transactions is also administered. This revealed that a portion of the payment for this amount was made by the deceased, Elvis Raja, through a fake company created by the three partners in crime. The data from the *Swift* Code bank files coincide with testimonies given by the collaborator with Justice, Qatip Jashari, and with the 'In' and 'Out' columns of the accountancy books of the trading company they set up between them. This money was transferred to Malta, and from there, into the account of another company in Columbia, the remainder of the payment making up the full price for the cocaine shipment was to be paid when the merchandise reached its destination…"

He leafed through several more pages and paused again to read something:

"… While the cocaine shipment had been ordered and the Columbian traffickers had dispatched it in the direction of Albania, the accused, Marjan Boja, purposely committed the execution of the banker in his rented apartment…the accused then failed in his attempt to murder another person, none other than his friend and associate, Qatip Jashari, but he did kill an innocent citizen and injured a child…Following the elimination of his two associates, the accused, Marjan Boja would have been the sole owner of the cocaine shipment, due to arrive at the port after a few weeks. His final aim was to appropriate all the profits for himself…" "

He had a swift look at the position of the citizen Asitrit Duka, who was with the accused on the night Elvis Raja was murdered. Apart from his testimony, the truth of this testimony was corroborated by the analysis of the mobile phone calls and other scientific expertise reports:

"…the result is that the mobile phone used in the communications between the accused, Marjan Boja, and the victim, Elvis Raja, on the night of the murder, is registered in the name of Atrit Duka. This phone with the number 066 715 8604, was used on 23 November 2018, at 23:40 hours, to contact the victim, Elvis Raja. The conversation lasted for 48 seconds. After the murder, the same mobile phone was given a new number, 066 845 2520, and it was used by Marjan Boja. It remained active up until 04:12:2018, a little after 10:12 hours. After that, neither the SIM card nor the telephone number were used again.

From this evidence, it clearly emerges that the new number installed by Marjan Boja in Astrit Duka-s mobile phone was used by him right up to the day of the attempt on Qatip Jashari's life.

He read the testimony given by witness Astrit Duka from beginning to end:

"…I only completed eight years of primary education and am unemployed. I live in the same neighbourhood as Marjan Boja; we go back years. I own an Audi number plate MN 313 GG. On 23 November, in the evening, Marjan Boja called and asked me if I would drive somewhere in connection with some job that he had to do. I recall it being a Friday. To begin with, around 22:00 hours, we had a coffee at a coffee bar near the stadium, where we chatted about insignificant things. I noticed he had his pistol on him. In fact, he always carried a gun. He was a person who knew many people; he had wide-ranging access. After 23:30, we got into my car, and I dropped him in the vicinity of the Presidency Building. On the way, Marjani used my mobile phone to call Elvis, his friend. He asked him to wait as he was heading in Elvis's direction. He told me to stay put and wait for him and that he had to meet someone. He walked off and headed into The Bloc. He didn't say who he was meeting, but from the phone call, I learned that he was meeting up with his friend, Elvis Raja, whom I had also met a couple of times with Marjan. I didn't ask him for details because I knew Marjan well. If you asked him about something sensitive, he would become violent, and it just didn't matter who was sitting opposite him then. He was away for around one hour. When he returned to the car, he was obviously in a hurry, and he told me to take the road toward the artificial lake. He said to speed it up because there was someone in Durres waiting for him. We accessed the ring road from the road running parallel to the dam on the artificial lake, and we were soon speeding along the motorway out to Durres. I dropped him off near "The Poplar Trees" in Durres. He told me to drop him off because he would stay there. He said he would hold on to my phone because he needed it. Of course, I accepted without a word. I handed him my phone. When he got out of the car, he instructed me to keep my mouth shut about the evening's movements. Then, I drove back to Tirana. I saw several police checkpoints set up at various intersections; at the "Zogu i Zi" intersection, I was also stopped, and my car was checked. I said I had had a few things to do in Durres and was on my way home. They let me through. When I got home, I saw on the news that there had been a murder that evening in The Bloc. The victim's name was not made public, but I immediately thought of Marjan. I have not told anyone about this. The next day, the victim's name was published in the media, and I knew, then and there, who had killed Elvis Raja. I haven't met Marjan Boja since then. I heard he was abroad, but I have not heard any other detailed information related to him. I can declare that on the night of the murder, he communicated with my phone, which he later took and never gave back. My phone was a Samsung, and my number, when I gave it to Marjan, was 066 715 8604."

Further on, Martin paused on reaching forensic evidence against the accused:

"…The testimony of the justice collaborator, Qatip Jashari, is accurate and verified by forensic experts. The samples of skin oils of the defendant Marjan Boja, documented when taken by experts, match the residue of his saliva lifted from a cigarette butt in the flat where Elvis Raja was murdered. The scientific reasoning reflected in the Biological Expertise Act clearly explains this…"

Looking through the details of the mobile phone call records, Martin felt a kind of excitement at the benefits of this invention - investigative phishing, now available to the whole world. Criminal organizations, with their various groupings, also tasted its fruits; the tracks they leave behind greatly alleviate the work of prosecutors. His mind wandered to the generations of prosecutors, not only in Albania but worldwide as if he wanted to pay his respects to that frontline of persons who battled against crime in very different circumstances, with no access to the infinite resources of research that exist today. *They're the heroes, not us, them! The "Cattani-s" of yesterday deserve a monument on the Moon, as the frontline resistance to crime which was born in tandem with man and has been his centuries-old co-traveler…*

Unexpectedly, he felt satisfied and content reading the indictment presentation, which was full of facts and details from electronic tabulations. This is why he made every effort to arrive at perfect interpretations, being the model of a person who abides by the laws of his country.

Further on, in re-reading the presentation of the indictment, he paused to focus on the records for taking information from the individual under investigation, dated 01:02:2019. The information was given by the accused, Qatip Jashari, who declared in part;

"…I was in Italy for several years. I returned from Italy in 2010. I set up a furniture business here in Tirana, which I have been dealing with since then. My business premises are near the train station. As regards the incident I was involved in on Tuesday, 4 December 2018, I wish to explain that I was ready to travel to Elbasan for work-related reasons. I was parked near the Faculty of Natural Sciences, and I was waiting for my friend, Marjan Boja, who had phoned me and asked me to wait at this spot as there was something he wanted me to do for him.

"…I had been friends with Marjan for years. While I was parked there waiting, someone drove up to my car on a motorbike and shot at me point blank. I don't remember a thing until I came to in the Military Hospital. When the police came to question me the first time in the hospital, I deliberately kept any suspicions I may have had to myself. I was certain about what had happened to me, but I thought I would wait until I got better and then go about solving my problems myself…"

"…Marjan Boja was the only person who knew I would be at that spot on the day of the incident. I was there, waiting for him to turn up. I had told him myself where I was. When I found out that Marjan Boja had killed our friend, Elvis Raja, then I was sure beyond a doubt that Marjan had wanted to get rid of me as well. In these circumstances, I decided to collaborate with you. Furthermore, I would like to explain that Marjan Boja took us on, Elvis Raja and I, in a seriously dangerous business undertaking. Unfortunately, we agreed to participate, chiefly because he was our friend and had our trust. Marjan had several connections in Italy and his friend in Columbia, and the plan was to bring in a large shipment of cocaine.

So, we're sitting in one of the private rooms of the "Safari" restaurant, and we have discussed this undertaking. Elvis had replied positively to Marjan's request that he, Elvis, provide three million dollars, which needed to be paid when the consignment was ready and before it was dispatched. Elvis was financially very wealthy. He owned a robust construction business and was the director of a bank branch. I agreed to find a facility on the outskirts of Tirana to store the goods and, later on, process them. Marjani would distribute and traffic to other countries because, as he maintained, he had open contact lines and was ready to move into action. Profits would be substantial, and in the end, Elvis's initial payment would be refunded. The profit from the sale of processed drugs was to be divided between us. The value, following processing, almost doubled. I was distraught when I heard about Elvis's murder, and I immediately phoned Marjan, but his mobile phone had been switched off. I believed that Marjan could glean more information on who had killed Elvis. He had connections everywhere, including the Police.

On the day of the attempt on my life, although the motorcyclist wore black shades, he did look like Marjan to me behind that silhouette that opened fire on me. Of course, I wanted to make sure. Now, it has all fallen into place for me; he eliminated Elvis, he tried to destroy me, and he would have been on his own. He would have received the consignment and managed the whole business on his own. He would be the sole boss and control all profits. This is why I decided to collaborate with justice and relate the truth regarding my involvement in this saga. I don't know whether Marjan had trafficked drugs beforehand. However, I speak with responsibility about the case that Marjan entrusted to Elvis and me to perform this job together, which almost cost both of us our lives…"

One other testimony was that of Arjana Boja, the defendant's mother:

Concerning the case, she testified:

"…I am the mother of Marjan Boja. On several occasions, my house has been raided by the Police, searching for my son, whom I have not set eyes on for months. He is abroad, he has phoned me from abroad and has told me that he is okay. I do not know if my son has committed a crime. What I do know is how hard it was to bring him up; I was on my own because there have been just the two of us since he was four. Marjan's father left for the United States and abandoned us both. He has never been in touch either with our son or me. Marjan indeed has behavioral problems, but I am unaware that he has caused anyone any harm…"

He focused on the final stand he advocated for the defendant, where he had written:

"…The same conduct Marjan Boja displayed toward the judicial police and the prosecutor he also displayed toward his defense lawyers. And now, he displays the same behavior before the panel of judges. In short, he does not accept the charges and shows no remorse for his crimes. He constitutes a serious threat to society…he has been examined regarding his mental state and was deemed responsible before the law…"

…From all the acts administered in the interests of these criminal proceedings and the evidence that was submitted to judicial examination, we conclude that:

"As regards what is presented above, in the final evaluation, it is proven, beyond all doubt, that in committing these crimes, the accused, Marjan Boja, collaborated with other persons; concisely, he was not on his own. We find the reasoning behind this final discussion firmly based on the Law and the evidence, and it concludes with the request for conviction of the defendant for the severe accusations presented at the outset and throughout the reading of the presentation of this indictment.

Honourable Judges,

We present a complete panorama of the criminal facts and conclude with the analysis of further evidence proving the guilt of the defendant, Marjan Boja.

…apart from the crime of international drug trafficking, which we gave a full account of above, the accused has also committed the crime of premeditated murder for his direct interest, where a mere attempt at assassination was out of the question for the defendant, as well as the crime of not possessing a license to carry a weapon.

In the case under discussion, the crimes for which the defendant is found guilty carry a high social risk, and the consequences were fatal; innocent citizens were killed; the transfer of narcotics from one state to another, a direct threat was posed to the legitimate interests of law and order and public safety. He had envisaged and desired these consequences of his activity.

Regarding mitigating circumstances, we declare that no such circumstances were announced during the investigation or adjudication.

At the end of the analysis and the evaluation of the evidence examined against the defendant, Marjan Boja, we conclude that it has been proven, beyond reasonable doubt, that he committed these grave crimes mentioned above. He committed these crimes intentionally and in collaboration, acts foreseen as grievous crimes, and consequently, he must be declared guilty.

Honourable Judges,

It is in the honour of this Court to pursue a severe criminal policy against the defendant with every conviction that you will bring peace to the soul of the families damaged by the homicide and to society at large, particularly of the youth and pupils, whom this defendant sought to poison, every day, with narcotics that he was going to distribute and traffic for the money, in this way constituting a real danger to the state.

For these reasons,

"I request that the defendant, Marjan Boja, be declared guilty and served a sentence of life imprisonment."

Although he had read it through several times to polish it here and there, Martin was now convinced that the final material was complete and fully substantiated. When his thoughts returned to the beginning of this criminal procedure, he recalled all the tension and despair he went through. The initial smokescreen thrown up around this process was never far from his mind. Now, he would also give a final response to public opinion and the media, who, for months, had been talking about "the power" of Marjan Boja and "the surrender" of the justice system in the face of this notorious figure of the crime world.

Sentencing a dangerous exponent of the world of crime to life imprisonment would not only be the main headline for the media but also a substantial signal to public opinion that law enforcement agencies are gaining ground in the fight against crime. This was only one case; they were working on dozens of other case files, all waiting to be solved, so at least all the silent and despairing anguish caused by killings or damages or losses could find closure and/or compensation. All hopes were pinned on the prosecutors whose office shelves, tables, and safes were bulging with files. These dossiers smouldered inside from the sheer weight of the sins and evil deeds all lurking in the lines and between the lines of the pages tied together and neatly filed away in compliance with standard protocol.

One of the most comprehensive and complete indictments was finished, a file that would shut the mouth of any judge and cause any defence counsel to surrender. Apart from anything else, he felt proud of all his colleagues' serious and professional work. An unexpected thought popped into his head: *How is it that no prosecutor in the world has ever won a Nobel Prize? Doctors, scientists, writers have, haven't they? Why can't a magistrate win one?.. Why are they not valued by the international commissions? Why are we overlooked when we are out there waging war against an evil of humanity? Why is that?*

He sat at his desk again, dismissing any feeling of ego for fame or public recognition. Let's get this trial over and done with first, then we can think about Nobel Prizes, Martin said and chuckled to himself.

He brought back to mind all the many pieces of legislation, interpretations, and legal analyses. They were endless. He believed that if all the laws in the world against human crime could be brought together, he would have created a pile two times the size of the globe, while if all these laws were arranged side by side, a massive net would span the globe and stretch out into space ensnaring all the stars. *"I am slightly daft,"* he said chuckling, *"but it gives me a feeling of satisfaction which only I enjoy, not any defendant, judge, or lawyer, just me.*

Martin Guri slammed the indictment presentation down on the table, all held together with metal clip organizers resembling a large slab of filleted meat. This was the longest indictment he had ever written before… "Like never before…" the words escaped his lips. He turned away from the table and fell into the armchair like a ship's anchor at berth, plummeting downwards to the sandy sea bed. He needed to be somewhere on the sea coast, looking up at the sun, his feet trailing in the water…He was sitting in an office of the state. He reclined back into the leather headrest of the armchair as if searching for peace. He felt weary to the bone. His eyes were riveted on the ceiling. *Whose was the office on the floor above?* This question had never occurred to him before. Had he ever been in the office above him before? He couldn't remember. Who wanted to know anyway?! He was a prosecutor and worked in the best conditions available; his office was as big as the hall where the long and tedious meetings of the Political Bureau of another time used to be held. It was from here that those top-secret bulletins used to be issued, and no one knew just who the next "enemy group" would be. He wondered what the hell brought that past to mind.

The building was constructed like the Steel Works was many years ago. Massive, somber. It was the largest building of the state administration. Staring up at the ceiling, he repeated the question: *Whose is the office above mine?* He seemed to picture the indictment presentation spread out all over the ceiling, page after page, letter after letter. Sentences shaped as scattered clouds drifted above the prosecutor's head…His gaze honed in on the one corner where a spider had spun its web. It was almost invisible. The spider must have retreated into a crack somewhere, waiting for its next prey, like the presentation which, in Martin's imagination, floated around on the ceiling above his head. Instinctively, he felt fear. For a second, he thought, what if the very last sentence of the indictment became entangled in the spider's web? *No, no!* He almost screamed! The assistant rushed into the room. "What is it, Chief? Are you alright?!" Martin placed a hand on his forehead and scratched his head. He signaled to the assistant to withdraw and close the door. This was the first time something like that had happened to him. But he wasn't worried. Again, he looked up to the corner of the ceiling where the spider web was. *The spider is the only insect that spins lethal webs, catching cousins of its ilk. It is a very serene way of hunting. No bloodshed, no tackling, perhaps even no pain. Like the fisherman's nets that capture the small fry. The sharks circle, smirking. To Martin, the extensive connections of Marjan Boja were like the shadows of the spiders that spun the invisible web in which they tried to trap and corrupt him. He pushed all of this out of his mind like shaking off a nightmare. Why don't the wolves and the jackals hunt like spiders? What about the lions in their hunting grounds in Africa? Why do they rip their prey asunder?!...*

Deep in thought, Martin Guri suspected he was experiencing a moment of teetering on the brink of a nervous breakdown. He had never lost his mind to such ramblings before in the innumerable court trials he had assisted on. What was happening to the prosecutor?!..

Chapter X
"Presentation of the Indictment before God"

Even with all the efforts of Eliza and their two sons to draw him into the folds of their habitual family humour, fun, and warmth, Martin remained as aloof and cold as he was when he walked through the door late in the afternoon on that day.

For Eliza and the children, the following day, a Friday on the verge of Spring, would usually have meant a family stroll or perhaps even a trip somewhere outside of Tirana and returning on Sunday afternoon. Understanding the tremendous workload of her husband, contrary to usual practice, Eliza said to Martin that once the trial was over tomorrow, they should go down south for a couple of days so that he could rest and recharge his batteries. All Martin had said was a dry, " Well, let's see," and made a show of playing with the boys. They both acted as if everything was normal; they didn't want their father to understand that they sensed and saw that he was suffering. *"The light of my eyes,"* he thought as he watched his sons trying to perk up his spirits.

In his childhood, he remembered seeing a film in the cinema called, "Cinderella." There was this fairy Godmother, who had a magic wand and, with a wave, turned pumpkins into horse-drawn carriages and rabbits into horses. He went back to the cinema three times to see that film.

In his case, black magic had happened. A specter of the past had swept into his office, instantly transforming it into a prison cell and him into a block of ice. As he gazed at his children and Eliza, the distorted, elongated images of Arjana and Marjan appeared, flitting and weaving in and out of all the rooms and passageways in the house, wherever he turned his gaze.

The closer the day and hour of the presentation of the indictment in Court drew nearer, the more defined the specters of the pair seemed to become in every nook and cranny of the house. At one moment, as he stood looking out of the window at Mt.Dajti in the distance, he thought he saw them standing on the summit of the mountain, eyes bulging, looking down with so much contempt, scorn, terror, and mockery.

Somewhat later on, he asked forgiveness of his wife and children and withdrew to his work studio. Contrary to the office-prison, where he was the prosecutor, and rightly so, in this smaller environment, he was the man-cum-prosecutor, and here, emotions often dominated over the law. It was here he fought those inner, psychological battles to achieve perfection in measuring with the scales of Justice. Every time he managed to achieve a balance between the Rule of Law and Moral Rights, he would return home relieved, irrespective of the sentences proposed for the crimes committed. "At peace with myself and God."

As early as during his University years, but later on in life too, Martin researched and searched for justice in all forms manifested over the centuries and by different regimes.

At intervals, when finding himself mired in the face of inadequate Albanian legislation (which, for years, had been undergoing dramatic, transitional changes), Martin had resorted to the usage of relevance, typical examples, juridical arguments from countries of proficient experiences, brought to the fore by scholars of law.

Like medicine, justice, too, evolves and cannot remain inflexible when confronted with changes to the ways of life and the sophistication of the exponents of crime. One day, while conversing about the evolution of the figures of crime, a friend of Martin's told him about an Italian televised serial on Dante's "Divine Comedy." In one of the episodes, the judges found it challenging to provide definitions (judgments) on acts people had performed in this life and the place they had to allocate them in the afterlife - Hell, Purgatory, or Heaven." Some people had committed crimes; for example, they robbed banks with a computer, cheated at the Casino, stole data from personal phones, filmed and took photographs without authorization, etc. These types of crimes were not foreseen in the work written by Dante. So then, the judges ordered that Dante review the masterpiece because it was obstructing business…

At home and in the office, Martin always kept a bible close by, but not on show. Even though he was no regular church-goer, he liked to leaf through its pages. He had picked up from the Bible and biblical narratives that perfect and divine justice could only be administered by God. Those who work to establish order and punish crime on Earth are given leave by God to do so, to perform that duty with as much truthfulness, equality, and fairness as possible and without using the law to abuse. In the final account, God will administer final justice for all creatures on this Earth, criminals and punishers alike.

When Martin fell prey to the erotic advances of the teacher, Arjana, Albania did not recognize religion and was a self-declared atheist country. Mulling this over in his mind, he felt a certain relief because perhaps he could be considered doubly innocent: firstly, he was an adolescent at the time, and someone, years his senior had duped, used, and abused him for personal interest (she raped me), and, secondly, in the celestial expanse of that time there was no God up above, but only a dictator, down below, with his criminal soldiers, like Arjana's husband. *At the time when Albania did not officially recognize religion, and the dictator had snatched away all the ascriptions to the Lord, could this be considered a moment frozen in time? Or, regardless of this and all the head-in-the-sandness, nothing replaces the existence of the Creator, no matter what the official declarations say?* No matter how the relationship with the Creator is evaluated, in essence, he was a minor who had been raped. In another democratic time, he could have reported this crime, and Arjana could have been condemned as she so richly deserved.

He turned on his side in the wide armchair he kept in his den for evenings when he wanted to continue working late into the night and where he often chose to sleep, not wanting to wake anyone up. His mind was on the next day, and, in particular, he wondered where he would be at this time tomorrow evening, twenty-four hours from now: at home, in the office, walking along the street, alone, on the news, discredited, dead, having committed suicide, dead, as in killed, where?

*Whatever my fate, I will present this indictment and seek the penalization of this person…*Martin said to himself…*this person.* It was the first time he did not say "of this criminal." Notwithstanding the circumstances, deep down inside, Martin was attempting to accept that part of his blood, albeit "contaminated." Having surrendered to the centrifugal force of self-judgment and level-headed analysis, Martin asked himself the following question: "What if Arjana had gone to see him one day, as she did, and with maternal insight and gratification had told me that my biological son, Marjan Boja, had become an artist, a rising star in America, would I have hated him? Would I have rejected and despised Marjan so profoundly? What if this biological son of mine had turned out to be a powerful and law-abiding businessman in Canada? Would I have agreed to talk to him?

What if he and his mother, Arjana, asked for a meeting with me without expecting me to break up with my family? What if it were sufficient for them to meet with me without expecting anyone else to be let in on it? In short, if he hadn't been criminal Marjan Boja, but Marjan Boja the intellectual, would I be agonizing so much over accepting him? Other questions seethed in my mind, like tiny insects pricking me inside and out.

These questions and the conversation he had with Martin-man and not Martin-prosecutor were sufficient to reach the first and most important decision: As his accidental father, tomorrow, I will not read the presentation of the indictment with the passion and aggressiveness I had planned to use. In other words, I would drain myself from all the toxins and the hatred I had accumulated for this and different types of criminals; even the grief I feel for Artur, my brother, murdered by someone just like Marjan, I will suppress inside myself and will not reveal it in the courtroom. I will delete from my memory all the negative emotions and burdens I have borne during these past months, particularly from the gestures and insinuations Marjan has thrown at me.

In that courtroom, I will do my best to remain an official, a servant of the Law. I will read out all the evidence implicating a citizen crime, who is considered innocent until found guilty. I should also consider him as "innocent" until the judges decide. Moreover, I will take care, even as an exception, that Marjan Boja is treated with dignity and fairness. I would have done this even without all the threats and ultimatums of his mother, even only taking into account the reasonable doubt that I am his biological father...

Continuing this cold-hearted analysis, the next batch of questions crowded his mind: *What if Arjana, just as she lied to her husband Zambak, that Marjan was his son, what if she lied to me as well and is blackmailing me, claiming Marjan is my son? Indeed, I slept with her several times, but where is the proof that she fell pregnant with me? What is to stop me from thinking that she slept with other men after me? Apart from a DNA test, nothing else proves I have anything to do with Marjan Boja. Nonetheless, this had-been trickster, "lethal beauty," music teacher, Arjana, knew from the outset, before coming to my office, that I, in the circumstances created, would not dare and that there was no public reason for me to make such a comparative analysis with an offender. I will always doubt whether what Arjana said to me was the truth, the same as I will forever be in a Hamletian dilemma: am I or am I not Marjan Boja's biological father? But whichever way things go, whatever happens, I am now compelled to extend some anonymous guardianship in the direction of this person in the prisons where he will serve his sentence. This "keeping an eye out for him" will be more demanding for me now than a mechanical doctoring of the files that Arjana wanted me to do. Let's say, for example, I tweaked the file to the extent that Marjan would be released after a few months in prison. This would suffice for Arjana to feel content with her son's regained freedom, with a son who will once again take to the road of crime, intensifying assaults and extending the proportions of human tragedies. But, all the same, let's follow her line of reasoning through to the end, the fulfillment of her request, based on the belief that Marjan will turn over a new leaf and will look after his mother, becoming a family man and giving his mother the joy of grandchildren.In this case, the primary concern is, where will I be in the future, in relation to Marjan Boja, now that his mother declared that I am his biological father? I am human, not a drawer that can be locked with a key. If I sever that fine thread of the law by doctoring the dossier of this individual, I can't sever that almost invisible thread that keeps me bound to the individual. The mere suspicion that I am his biological father will be sufficient to make me suffer all my life, in one way or another. So this is the most significant damage and blow this woman has dealt me. To resolve one problem, she created another, even more devastating problem, and in her efforts to save one person, she is simultaneously hanging two!*

He tried hard to recall a similar case, even theoretical, but failed. *This is a one-in-a-million case; there may have been a similar case, but it would be impossible to find...*

Martin reached for the Bible on a little cherry-wood bedside table. He turned the small lamp on, intent on finding perhaps a passage that resembled his predicament. Leafing through the pages, he came across a few sheets of paper folded in half; they were notes he had jotted down at a biblical conference at which the well-known American Pastor Erwin W. Lutzer had spoken. This activity was held in Tirana over four weeks ago, and he attended it with Eliza. As was his habit, Martin had taken notes from Pastor Lutzer's contribution, chiefly concerning justice and the heavenly assessment of it. Martin was curious to reread some of the excerpts with an inner urge and diabolical apprehension. He wanted to find out just how current the interpretations of the pastor might be in the mess he was in. He began to read about the need for neutral justice.

That shocked him to the core. The words seemed to be just what the doctor ordered! They were like magic words deliberately sent to him on this pitch-black night without the glimmer of light at the end. He read on and sensed a kind of reconciliation and peace with himself as if God was sitting beside him.

He paused in his reading of the notes he had made and pondered about impunity, the consequences of which lead to the growth of crime and political intervention (in this case, Arjana and Marjan's criminal ties) to prevent penalization for crimes committed. So, to a certain extent, Marjan Boja had escaped penalization precisely because he had never been penalized during his journey. Ever since the very first crime he committed, he had never been penalized. If he had been taken into custody and properly penalized for his initial crime, there is a good chance he would have quit the road of crime. But now, here he is, facing the risk of being dealt a life sentence!

"Administering humane justice is a particularly difficult undertaking, but our goal should be to equally administer justice," Pastor Lutzer said in his contribution.

…Further on, Martin read, "We have repulsed justice and repelled honesty far off into the distance. because truth is hampered in the public domain! It is said that truth cannot get in. The truth is missing. So, with the absence of truth, we cannot have justice…Martin Luther, centuries later, discovered that there was a justice that derived from God, and this justice is gifted to those who repent for their sins and believe. In other words, the Lord's standard is very high, and we can never know whether we can reach it or not…"

Cautioning that the rapport of people with justice is one of the most challenging rapports, Pastor Lutzer emphasized that no matter how perfect state institutions may be, or those of justice, they cannot replace God. "If you say that we must always obey government, then what you are saying is that government is your God. If I believe that the United States Supreme Court is the sublime authority, then what I am saying is that the Supreme Court is God himself. Show me your law's source, and I will show you your Gods."

Among other things, in his notes on the contribution, Martin's attention was drawn by a brief story that Lutzer related to illustrate justice and equality before the Law. He spoke about how an American citizen was fined one hundred dollars for breaking the law while driving his car. The fine had to be paid at the Court on the appointed day. However, due to his financial circumstances, when the citizen appeared in Court he had no money to pay the fine. Moreover, he was also senior of age. After reading the police report, the judge told him he had to pay one hundred dollars immediately, and he would be free to go. Under no circumstances could the fine be excused. The citizen repeatedly told the judge that he could not pay it because he did not have a single dollar. So, according to Lutzer's words, "the judge stepped down from his bench, removed his judge's robes, put on his everyday jacket and approached the accused slipping one hundred dollars into his pocket. He then returned, put the robes of a judge back on, and addressed the accused: You owe the state

100 dollars. I know you don't have it, but I have observed that someone has paid for you." The law, as the foundation of the state, was defended, and the dignity of the citizen, as the foundation of society, was protected! And who did the more significant part of the job? None other than the man of justice!

Martin was now lucid. Tomorrow morning, he must defend the law, be impartial, and view justice through the eyes of the law and the eyes of humane ethics. The Prosecution is not God, and the Constitution is not the Holy Bible, but neither am I a target to be sacrificed for the crimes of Marjan Boja. After all is said and done, the criminals must be punished. As for every sin I have committed, I will be responsible to God alone.

***

Eleven o'clock on the dot. The curtain was rising on the trial, probably the most closely covered by the media and talked about in Albanian society. Prosecutor Martin Guri was to be the quintessential element of the day. He entered the courtroom with a steady stride and the sensation that he was the center of attention. He sat down and arranged his manuscripts on the side of the accused, to the right of the bench where the judges would sit, opposite the podium where the lawyers were seated. The last forty-four hours had taken a huge toll on him spiritually, but he had worked very hard on himself to be ready morally and professionally. He strove hard to keep it together; he had to rise to the level of performance expected of him. He represented the charges brought by the state and the law. He wore a black suit, white shirt, and dark blue tie. The robe of the prosecutor, worn over what was a very official attire anyway, lent grace to his figure.

In that courtroom, in front of everyone, he was to present the most significant indictment of his career; the thought

171

suddenly flashed through his mind, "Without killing crime, there is no future"!, although capital punishment does not exist in Albania. The perpetual conflict of thoughts seemed to gnaw away at him and weaken him from within. He had never felt these misgivings before, in his entire career, prior to the final discussion of a case. Emotionally, spiritually, and mentally, he was way overcharged, while at the same time, he strove to lend weight to his position and responsibility as a prosecutor of the state. As the parties filed into the courtroom and took their seats, Martin mused:

Which is the spawning ground of this world of crime? Is it us or them? Why did a "biological morsel" of mine transmute into a criminal? Should an accusing finger be pointed as much at me as the criminal, Marjan Boja? What about the ones who lay down the law and plant the seeds of anarchy and chaos? Why are they missing from my indictment? Should I go back over the presentation?... Should this court sitting be postponed?...

Martin felt the beads of perspiration break out caused by these troubled thoughts. He was conscious that he had to conceal these thoughts that had tortured him so much. All he had to do was focus on the indictment and lying on the bench top of the podium; it was like an invitation to see justice done.

Hushed stillness. The weight of this silence hung like the concrete hood of a bunker suspended over the courtroom. From one of the side doors, the panel of judges filed in with a solemn step. A curt command was barked out:

- The judges have entered, all rise!

Martin felt the cold sweat break out. He had never experienced this kind of spiritual and physical turmoil before. He glanced over at the cage, and through its bars, he made out Marjan Boja with that nasty and ironic smirk stamped on his features. He turned and looked out over the courtroom and opposite him, sitting in the right-hand corner, he caught sight of Arjana. Their eyes met. There she was, seated towards the back rows. Those pale features highlighted her eyes. At this distance, he couldn't discern that killer look he had encountered when she burst into his office. Her black clothing and hair made her resemble a declining sorceress. He didn't realize, but he was staring at Arjana. Her face seemed so shriveled and wasted.

The Chief Judge did the formalities of declaring the sitting open and introduced the parties in the case. He ordered courtroom security to ensure that there would be no recording or filming either by camera or mobile phone. The session was not open to the public, with the exception of those seated in the court room.

The big wall clock showed 11 hours and 11 minutes.

"The Prosecution has the floor," his voice boomed.

From the large windows of the courtroom, Martin could see the sky that appeared to be like an extension of the courtroom's ceiling. He stood up and began speaking calmly. He occasionally looked up Between sentences and paragraphs, and instinctively, his gaze would travel from Marjan to Arjana. Slowly but surely, his voice took on the right tempo; the resonance of his words became more emphatic, deeper, and more imposing. Now, he was trying to interpret and not merely read a cold text. An astonishing surge of daring erupted from within him, delivered with skillful drama, energy, undauntedness, and elation. His interpretation was lengthy. One after the other, he went through the episodes, presented the evidence, and juridically analyzed the crimes, the killings, the acts…He explained everything in that presentation, down to the smallest detail.

The courtroom, the judges, lawyers, the defendant, the security officers, everyone listened spellbound, following the voice that reverberated throughout the quietness of this dignified room. This presentation of an indictment was unique. It took a long time to read out this highly complicated, multifaceted, and voluminous statement. And Martin Guri knew that he had never presented a statement in this manner before. Casting an eye over his audience, time after time, Martin realized he held them in the palm of his hand. The whole time, there was not a whisper from anyone. It was plain to see that not even the judges, the lawyers, or anyone else in the courtroom had ever experienced this kind of pathos and such convincing truthfulness. What defense would the defense lawyers bring against this indictment? A dark shadow had fallen over Marjan Boja's face. The ironic smirk was gone. It was futile that Arjana pinned her hopes on the notion that the past would save the future.

When approaching the end, Martin lifted his head from the papers he clutched in his hand, and his gaze roamed the room. He paused, looking over at Arjana. That washed-out face of hers seemed to loom before him. He remembered the first instant she had drawn him to her body, and he was a most inexperienced adolescent. That moment of bitter-sweet biological defilement that had produced Marjan Boja. An irrational folly of youth that reared its ugly head after so many years in its most vengeful form. His mind raced, and he considered shouting at the top of his voice and accusing Arjana. He had the urge to shout it to the skies: *I accuse the defendant's mother of abuse against myself. She raped me, she took advantage of me. Using her power to bait me, she misappropriated biological matter that bred birthright and brought a monster into this world whom I want nothing to do with. Here, publically, I accuse…*

He was no longer speaking. Martin stood there, like those Roman statues, nude, with their marble genitals on full display as rudiments of the time. He had fallen silent before the judges and the courtroom, where everyone looked like Marjan to him. The silence continued, and Martin, like the pendulum of a clock, swung his gaze from Marjan to Arjana. They are identical, mother and son, the stuff of criminals. Both of them should be sentenced here and now…Someone could be in the audience, sent by the bosses who hand-delivered that letter to him. He didn't know them, and under no circumstances did he ever want to meet them. Like hyenas, they slunk into sight everywhere. Even in their inducing, these shadows ushered in death. Perhaps they would undertake further steps. They had failed in their first attempt. They were getting confirmation of that in today's indictment. This indictment constituted Martin's public response to that letter they had delivered to his office.

Martin was fighting for self-control.

- Prosecutor, please continue delivering your statement.

He made a superhuman effort to gather his wits together, finding the strength to push on. The presentation of the indictment had to be closed. The prosecutor ended his statement with renewed energy resembling the deep rumblings of a hitherto dormant volcano.

- Honoured members of The Bench of Judges! Based on the evidence and in-depth analysis presented here, I ask the honored Bench that the defendant, Marjan Boja, be sentenced to life imprisonment.

He paused slightly, inhaled deeply, and added:

- If possible, I would ask for more…but the law is the law.

The courtroom was in shock. Such an explosive indictment was very rare. Martin sat down and looked out over the courtroom. He noticed Arjana, who was staring over at him, frozen.

Like a bomb, Martin Guri had launched this dossier, the statement, along with all the evidence, into the courtroom, at the defendant, the lawyers, and the judges draped in the black robes of the law. When Martin finished, the judges exchanged looks of perplexity. The power and the might of the Prosecutor had reached a point.

The Chair of the sitting was just about to announce the continuation of the session when there was a hysterical outburst in the middle of the room as if it originated from the floor:

"Nooo, noo, Prosecutor, you are the criminal! Marjan is our son…Nooo!!

Martin recognized the voice but did not budge from his seat. His eyes came to rest on the insignia engraved into the wall, "Justice for All." He looked back at the courtroom and saw Arjana, who had collapsed to her knees after emitting that howl; slowly, she fell to the floor. He could no longer see her; she had been swallowed up by the rows of seats and the people in the courtroom. Then came another howl:

- We need help here, help!

The sitting was closed. Confusion broke out on the floor of the courtroom. Martin Guri had remained frozen in his chair. He had done what had to be done. When he came to, he noticed that the Ambulance medical staff had arrived on the scene. They had come to take Marjana, lying, stretched out on the courtroom floor. Martin began massaging his limbs; the feeling had drained out of them. His eyelids drooped heavily; he was totally washed out. When he opened his eyes, he saw he was still sitting there, alone. The cage with its criss-cross iron bars was empty. His gaze dulled.

"Prosecutor, prosecutor"! His assistant was tugging at his arm. He shook himself and opened his eyes wide.

"What happened, the Statement…"?! Martin mumbled, looking around as if in a trance.

"That's all over and done with now, Prosecutor! Here's the whole statement: in my bag," his assistant explained, opening up the bag he was holding.

"Where is the defendant? Where did the judges go? What about Arjana?" Martin asked in a haze. His assistant fell silent for a split second. For the first time, he felt pity for the person he adored. He couldn't understand this weakness.

"They have just notified us that she is still unconscious; they're rushing her to the hospital."

"She's alive?"

"Barely, they said there was little hope, though," the assistant replied.

"Poor woman, she couldn't bear the pain, could have been a heart attack, perhaps," Martin said, rummaging around in his bag.

"What did she say about me"? Martin ventured.

"She didn't say anything, Prosecutor, nothing at all. No one understood what she was saying; she kept screeching as if possessed."

Straining to hold it together, although he felt he was on the brink of passing out, Martin said to his assistant, "Please, take care that the confidentiality of the Statement is preserved and secure. I'm heading out."

Martin Guri gave the young man a confused look, turned around, and left. He walked out of the courtroom without a second glance back.

I need to rest, he muttered, taking the pathway through the park. He walked at a free and leisurely pace and felt lighter in spirit. He threw his head back, and his gaze dissipated into the blueness of the sky. He loosened his tie and took a deep breath. At one of the park's corners, a motorbike carrying two people wearing full-face cycling helmets rolled past him. As soon as they were close enough, one of them drew a pistol and opened fire, hitting him multiple times. The shots were muffled, deafeningly quiet. Martin fell to the ground, face first, in the dirt.

Two passers-by who witnessed the scene ran for their lives, terrified. An elderly lady approached, wailing and screaming; she dropped to her knees beside Martin, taking his head in her hands and turning it toward her. There seemed to be a serene smile imprinted on his face; the elderly lady called out to a boy on a bike, "Hey, stop a minute son, come and give me a hand here? It looks to me as if he has gone…I could be wrong, though; maybe there is still hope…"

THE END